Save Me

Broken People Duet Part Two

Vi Carter

Contents

OTHER BOOKS BY VI CARTER

Other Books by VI CARTER

<u>WILD IRISH SERIES</u>
FATHER (FREE)

VICIOUS #1
RECKLESS # 2
RUTHLESS #3
FEARLESS #4
HEARTLESS #5

<u>THE BOYNE CLUB</u>
DARK #1
DARKER # 2
DARKEST #3
PITCH BLACK #4

<u>THE OBSESSED DUET</u>
A DEADLY OBSESSION #1
A CRUEL CONFESSION #2

<u>YOUNG IRISH REBELS</u>
MAFIA PRINCE #1
MAFIA KING #2

MAFIA GAMES #3
MAFIA BOSS #4

MURPHY'S MAFIA MADE MEN
SINNER'S VOW #1
SAVAGE MARRIAGE #2
SCANDALOUS PLEDGE #3

WARNING

This book is a dark romance. This book contains scenes that may trigger some readers and should be read by those only 18 or older.

CHAPTER ONE

JARED

*B*LOOD.

I'm staring down at the stark red liquid flowing across the white tiles. I can't look away as the warm liquid pools around my bare feet. I'm tempted to step back, but I'm captivated as it makes a path around me. It's like water. I see my reflection in the blood. The light is dim in my parents' bathroom, but I can still make out my face. A vibration races across the liquid, and my image wavers. My eyes travel a little further ahead. His chunky silver watch catches the light, and before I can raise my gaze any higher, the world turns dark. The image before me disappears, and I am airborne as my mother lifts me from the tiled floor of the bathroom. The scent of her Eternity perfume surrounds me. My feet are still warm. I want to tell her about the red liquid that I stepped in.

"Keep your eyes closed, Jared." Her voice is a whisper as she sits me on a soft bed. She leaves me, and I do as she says. I keep my eyes closed. Behind my lids, the red liquid keeps repeating in my mind. A warm cloth touches my feet, and I want to look, but once again, I obey her.

"You're a good boy." My mother's voice wobbles. "You're my good boy." Her hands shake as she tugs on a pair of socks over my damp feet. When she pushes on my shoes, I peek at her with one eye. She's still in her pajamas, and so am I.

I want to ask her what's happening. "Why are you sad?"

Tears stream down her face. She tilts her head and touches my face. For a moment, through the upset and confusion, it's just us. I know how much she loves me. She knows how much I love her.

Voices from the hall have her gaze shifting, but not before her eyes fill with dread.

Something in me feels unsettled. I want my dad.

My mother rises and blocks me as the bedroom door opens.

"Master Jay." A hand touches my shoulder. I'm snapped back to the present and look down at Layla. I'm on the ground, and she's in my arms. My fingers are coated in her blood. Her face is ghastly white.

"The ambulance is on its way, Master Jay."

I can't speak. I can't separate the memory from what's happening in front of me. I press down on the wound on Layla's shoulder, which oozes too much blood. The blood continues to pool around us, and my mind keeps jumping to my parents' bathroom. I have no idea where that came from. How old was I? Five or six? I've often tried to remember what my mother looked like, but nothing has ever been as clear as that memory. I have photos, but that's all they are. Photos of a woman they say was my mother.

I take one hand off Layla's wound as I reach for her neck. "Layla." Her name comes out a pained growl. I search with my other hand for a pulse. It's there, but the beat is slow and slight. I hear heavy footsteps on the stairs like I did when I was a child. The footsteps were loud outside my parents' bedroom door that night. I lose my focus and blink as paramedics and the Gardaí reach us on the landing. It's now I notice that the lights are back on in the hallway. I look to where Chester once stood, like I expect him to be there smiling. But the space is empty.

Too many people flood around us, and I'm moved aside as they lift Layla onto a stretcher. I'm staring at the blood that stains my hands. It seems to have flowed into every groove and crescent, tainting me.

"Master Jay." William stands over me, and two Gardaí wait by his side.

I stop staring at my hands and get off the floor.

"You want to tell us what happened?" the first Gardaí asks, and they all seem to lean in. Others move around the space. Are they searching for a weapon? Do they think I did it?

I look at William and wonder how much he saw, what he knows. Did he see where Chester went after he shot Layla?

I tighten my jaw as I glare back at the Gardaí. They're fucking laughable. Justice will never be served at their hands. How many nights did I pick up the phone, dial 999, and start to report what was happening, only to have them ask for my name and address? Stupid stuff. *Where are you? How old are you? Are you alone?* Instead of listening to me.

"A man broke into my home and shot my girlfriend. Who I need to be with." I step aside and no one stops me as I race down the stairs. The lights from the ambulance illuminate the foyer with blue and red strobes. I'm too late. They're pulling away and taking Layla with them.

"Jay, what happened?" My father drops his suitcase and jacket on the floor and moves swiftly toward me. Fear twists his features as he grips my shoulders and looks me over.

"It's Layla. She was shot." My words are painful. "I need to be with her." I'm ready to step away from my father's grip when he tightens his hold on me.

"You need to take a moment."

I'm shaking my head. "You never liked her."

My father waves his hands in the air before placing them back on my shoulders. "Son, I would never wish this on anyone. If you are worried, I'm worried." His fingers sink a little deeper into my arms. "You don't want to go to the hospital covered in blood."

I frown, but as I look down at my shirt and jeans, I see I'm covered in Layla's blood. There's so much fucking blood.

I can't lose her.

My father must see the alarm that consumes me. "Trust me, go change. I'll get you a brandy and then take you there myself."

I'm turning back to the stairs. "I don't want a brandy. Have the car ready." I race up the stairs. It's like a fucking TV crime scene.

By the time I get changed and return to the landing, a forensics team has arrived. William meets my gaze and nods. "I'll stay here, Master Jay."

"Thanks." I keep going so the Gardaí can't stop me. My father stays true to his word and is in the car waiting for me.

Once he starts driving, he leans over and pops open the glove compartment. The brown liquid swishes in the brandy bottle. He doesn't say anything, but I take it out and uncap the lid. I don't ask why he has a bottle of brandy in his car. I take a few swallows before putting the lid back on.

"Why don't you tell me what happened, son?" His calming tone settles the frazzled panic inside me.

"We were talking. Layla was getting ready to go home." I glance at my father. "I need to tell Evelyn and Carl."

"They already know."

I want to ask how, when, and who told them, but it doesn't matter. "She went to the bathroom, and the lights went out. I went into the hall to see what was happening, and a man was there."

I uncap the bottle again and take a drink, knowing if I stay on this path, there is no coming off it. I had a chance to tell my father and report Chester to the Gardaí.

But it didn't feel like enough. Not after what he's done.

"He was looking for the safe. I told him I didn't have money."

My father meets my gaze. I can't decipher what I see, but the look disappears, and he nods. "You should have given him the money, Jay. Jesus, son, you could have died."

"I didn't think he was going to shoot me."

He tightens his hold on the steering wheel, and I keep watching him as I speak. "He raised the gun and got ready to take his shot. I was going to tell him where the safe was when Layla appeared. She stepped in front of me and..."

My father grips my arm. "We will get him," he reassures me.

I don't want them to get him. I'll do it myself.

We arrive at the hospital, and he parks the car while I go to the main reception area. The receptionist takes far too long to find out where Layla is, and my agitation is at its max. She's aware of my anger as I tower over her; her gaze keeps diverting to me, and her eyes widen.

"Got her." There's relief in her voice, but I don't feel it.

My father arrives at my side when we're motioned toward a waiting room. The minute I step in, I want to leave. Evelyn stands up from a row of blue plastic chairs, and she has a look of hate directed at us. Carl reaches out and takes her arm. He knows, I know, everyone in this room knows, that she blames me. It's written all over her fucking face.

She pulls away from Carl, and I don't react as I allow her hand to connect with my face.

"Why couldn't you just leave her alone?" Her hysterical words don't affect me, and when she reaches up to hit me again, I grip her arm.

"You brought her here, remember, Evelyn?"

"Get your hands off my wife." Carl stands tall beside her.

I don't like being told what to do. I don't release her.

"I think everyone needs to calm down." My father steps up beside me, and only then do I release Evelyn's arm. She's still staring at me like I'm Satan. "It was a robbery. This is no one's fault."

Evelyn finally looks away from me to my father, with the same level of hate in her eyes. She turns to Carl and starts to cry. "My beautiful daughter."

Carl consoles her. I try to give her a moment, but I want to know what's happening. They won't tell me anything, as I'm not blood related, though I'm more to Layla than these two combined.

"What did the doctor say?" I ask Carl.

Evelyn spins. "That our daughter was shot."

I step away from her. This is pointless. I turn to my father.

"I'll find out." He keeps his voice low as he leaves to get me answers. Money will make the doctors talk. I don't want to be left with Evelyn and Carl, but for Layla, I'll show some respect.

"If you need anything, just ask," I say.

"I don't want anything from you," Evelyn bites.

My frayed patience snaps. I face her fully. "You knew where I was, so let's not act innocent."

Evelyn's face fills with color.

"You wouldn't want Layla to know that you kept us apart all these years, would you?"

Carl steps closer to me. "Are you threatening my wife?"

I ignore him and try to reason with Evelyn. "I love her. I would never hurt Layla." I leave them with my parting words and wait in the hallway for my father to return.

Noise filters in from all angles, but it's a lonely fucking place. Very lonely, when my mind keeps replaying the scene in the bathroom. I'm trying to analyze everything about the memory I had earlier. Was it a memory? I have no idea where it came from, but it felt so real. I can remember the smell, sharp like iron, almost cold to my lungs.

I can almost taste my mother's smell in my mouth. I slide down the wall and place my head in my hands, hoping to erase some of the confusion. The watch I remember seeing on the lifeless wrist was my father's, which he still wears. Had he fallen? Was it some sort of accident? Did Layla's blood trigger the memory?

Layla.

When the gun went off and her blood hit my face, the world went blank. My mind, for a split second, fired too much at me, and I couldn't react to anything. I wanted to kill Chester. Take the gun from his fingers and make him eat the fucking bullets. I wanted to make sure Layla was okay. I wanted to close my eyes and pretend it wasn't happening. Instead, I sank to the ground with her, and my mind went somewhere else.

"Jay."

I rise quickly as my father returns. My heart hasn't slowed down, and it threatens to pound out of my chest. I'm shaking my head. She can't be dead, yet my father is wearing a look that terrifies me. The door behind me opens, and Evelyn comes out, pauses, and is ready to go back in.

"She's in an induced coma," he tells the room.

"What?" Evelyn's cry matches my internal fear. Carl arrives out of the waiting room. "How do you know that? Where is the doctor?"

My father keeps his composure as he delivers the news to me like we're alone. "Her blood loss was too severe, so they need to stabilize her in order to keep her alive."

Evelyn's cries drown out everything else, and I want to tell her to shut the fuck up.

"I want to see her," I say to my father. He doesn't answer, but he leaves, making my request a reality.

Evelyn's wails are enough to drive me from the hallway, but I stay where I am and try to find some sympathy for them. They've raised Layla and kept her safe. I owe them that much.

Clearly, they love her.

"She's strong. She'll make it," I try to reassure them.

It stops Evelyn from crying. She runs a hand across her face and tries to compose herself. "She's the strongest child I've ever known." Evelyn smiles through her pain, and I see the love there for Layla.

I nod.

"Did you see who did this?" Carl asks.

"It was dark. He cut off the electricity." I shake my head. "I wish I knew."

Evelyn steps away and returns to the waiting room. Carl doesn't follow her like I thought he would. Instead, he stays.

"It's not your fault, Jared. Evelyn doesn't blame you."

"She does."

Carl half smiles. "She does. But she's upset. She'll calm down."

There's an awkward silence, and Carl leaves me alone. I wait another twenty minutes. I'm close to searching the hospital for Layla's room when my father returns.

He glances over my shoulder as if looking to make sure I'm alone.

"They're in the waiting room," I say and nod my head in the direction Evelyn and Carl went.

He nods, and I see something close to pride shine in his eyes. "You can see her."

CHAPTER TWO

LAYLA

I'M SWIMMING IN A sea of darkness. At times, I hear voices before I get swallowed up and the voices dim.

"You know, when you first came home, you never slept in your bed. You would mess the quilt up and make it look like you did…"

A soft laugh that I recognize soothes me.

"I used to go into your room in the middle of the night, and you would be bundled up on the floor under the bed with one of Carl's sweaters. And in the morning, you would be back in your own bed, the sweater nowhere in sight."

Silence stretches, and the murky water swallows me again. The woman's voice doesn't stop, and when I break the surface of pain and mist, she's still there, still talking.

"I never really liked him, to be honest." She pauses. "The flowers he keeps sending are divine." Another pause. Her voice grows muffled as I sink, but I want to stay with Evelyn. I want to know who she's talking about. Who is sending me flowers, and why?

"It's been days, and he hasn't left. I think he's sleeping in the room next to yours. He takes up most of the visiting times." I hear the fondness in Evelyn's voice even as she tries to hide it.

"He doesn't say much." She grows distant, and heat behind me has me turning in my dark pool. A red hot wave moves too quickly, bringing with it pain that has me screaming.

"Get a doctor! Help!" Evelyn's screams follow me until I'm pulled deep under the water. Long seconds pass, and it feels as though I've been submerged there before I break the surface.

Only this time, I return to silence. No one is speaking, but there's movement. His smell triggers an image of Jared's handsome face, and with it comes a want. A yearning that aches. I want to see him. I want to kiss him.

Jared.

I float and he never speaks, but he stays for a while. I want him to talk, but he doesn't.

"I think the whole school is out in the waiting room."

I perk up at Evelyn's voice. *Where is Jared?*

"I met Ashley. I can see why you like her. She's such a sweetheart, and Nicco." I can hear the smile in Evelyn's voice.

Her hand touches mine and pulls me higher out of the water. "I prayed for a child and God gave me you. I'm praying to Him again to give me back my baby." A kiss is pressed against my cheek, and moisture seeps down my face. "Come back to your mother."

Mother.

Her tears pull me higher, and I want to return to Evelyn, my mother. I want to comfort her and tell her it will be okay, but I'm sinking again.

Then the dark water consumes me.

***

Why is someone shining a light in my face? I raise my arm, which is as heavy as lead, managing to get my hand close to my eyes. The light dims, but something pulls on my arm.

"Careful. You'll pull out your needle."

My eyes flitter open at Jared's voice, only to slam closed again. The light is too bright. "The light," I croak.

My words send a whoosh of Jared's breath across my face.

"They said you might not be able to talk," he says, his voice growing more distant as he moves away. A rattle of metal ceases, along with the bright light. I blink. My vision isn't clear.

Jared returns to my side, and it takes me a few more attempts to focus as he slowly comes into view. He's growing a beard. He appears older. He doesn't touch me.

"Why wouldn't I be able..." I stop to moisten my lips. Jared picks up a drink and brings it to my mouth. I take a small swallow. Once I'm done, I try to piece together what's happening. "Where am I?"

My body aches, especially my shoulder.

"You're in the hospital." Jared places the drink back on the bedside table. He stays standing, and there's something standoffish about him.

I'm trying to jog my memory, but I can't seem to recall what happened. I squeeze my eyes tight as it slowly trickles back in. I was at Jared's house. We took a walk in the garden.

"You were shot."

I try to sit up, but the pain keeps me lying down. "Shot?"

"You lost so much blood, Layla. They had to put you into an induced coma."

Coma?

"For how long?" How much time has passed?

"Ten days."

The door rattles, and someone knocks on the top glass portion. I can't see who it is, as the blind has been drawn.

"Do you remember anything?" Jared doesn't even look at the door. He's speaking like no one has knocked.

I try to think of Jared's house. All I remember is having a picnic. Our time in the garden. Moving inside his house, and the lights going out. "It's fuzzy."

The banging on the door grows more insistent.

"There was a robbery at my house. The gunman fired, and you stepped in front of me." Jared speaks in a monotone voice.

He's watching me, waiting for my response. The knocking stops.

"I was shot," I repeat. My fingers glide along the bandage. "I don't remember."

Dark circles under Jared's eyes have me wanting to ask if he's okay. I swallow the dryness in my throat. The knocking returns, and Jared leaves my bedside. He pulls his navy jacket off the back of a chair. I watch as he crosses the room, opens the door, and lets the doctor and two nurses in. He doesn't stop as they question why the door was locked.

The room is a fluster of activity as I'm checked, poked at, and asked too many questions. My mind is snagged on Jared. There's something he isn't telling me.

A squeal from Evelyn has me finally letting go of Jared for now. She makes her way to my bedside, and the doctor stands aside to let her close to me. She hugs me gently, and her cries are pressed into my neck.

"You're awake!"

Carl walks to the opposite side of the bed and takes my hand.

"I'm sorry I scared you."

Evelyn breaks the hug. "How are you feeling?"

Before I can answer, Evelyn turns to the doctor. "How is she? Is there any damage? She seems fine." Evelyn reaches down and grabs my other hand as she fires questions at the doctor.

The doctor smiles kindly and holds up a hand. The nurses check stats, but their smiles are there too.

"We can't say for certain, but so far, it's looking really good." For the first time, the doctor looks at me. "You are a very lucky girl. I'm confident you'll make a full recovery."

I nod and force a smile, like this isn't weird. What happened to me? I wish I could remember.

"When can she go home?" Evelyn releases my crushed fingers, and I find myself looking up at Carl. His gaze is filled with tears, and he squeezes my hand softly.

"We need to keep her here for a few days for observation. If everything is clear, she can go home then."

Evelyn looks at me with a huge smile. "Thank God."

The doctor and nurses leave. Evelyn doesn't ask me questions about what happened. She keeps fussing with the blankets and pillows. Food arrives, and I eat a little under Evelyn's supervision. Carl sits down, and after an hour or so, he puts on the TV. He doesn't watch what plays out on the screen. He's too busy watching me like I might disappear.

They keep looking at me like it's a miracle I'm here. Maybe it is.

The day dwindles on, and I keep falling in and out of sleep. Each time I open my eyes, Evelyn is hovering over me. It takes Carl pulling her away for food to get her out of the room. I feel terrible, but when they leave, I sit up with relief. The distance gives me a moment to try to figure out what's happening.

I touch my bandaged shoulder, and pain ignites quickly. The memory of a bang of a gun has me snapping my eyes shut. Someone shot me.

A shiver assaults me. The door opens, and once again, I get a wash of relief that it isn't Carl and Evelyn. The doctor enters with a soft smile that lights up his eyes, which are framed with black glasses.

"How are you feeling?"

"Confused. Tired. Sore."

He nods at each word. "That's normal. Have you had any memory loss?"

"Yes. I don't remember what happened."

He nods again and moves closer to my bed. "That's normal as well. In most cases, memories return. And it's looking good, Layla."

"Thank you."

"The Gardaí are here to ask a few questions. If you don't feel up to talking, I can send them away."

It doesn't matter. "I don't remember what happened."

"I'll tell them to come back another day." The doctor smiles again before leaving the room.

I drift into a light sleep. At some point, Evelyn and Carl return, and their whispered words float around me.

"Jared, she's awake. She came out of the coma, and they don't think there are any long-term injuries." Evelyn's voice carries a note of hostility.

I open my eyes slightly. Jared closes the door. He's freshly shaven, and my stomach quivers at the sight of him in the room. His black clothing and hooded gaze make him appear dangerous.

"That is great news," Jared responds.

He doesn't tell them he was here when I woke up. Jared looks right at me, and I open my eyes fully. I want to ask where he was. Why did he leave, and why is he acting so off? I don't ask any questions.

He greets Carl, and the room grows silent.

"Are you okay?" I ask Jared as I try to sit up.

Carl and Evelyn move at the same time to help me sit up.

"I'm fine," I reassure them, but Carl lifts me while Evelyn stacks my pillows behind my back. They're both so careful with me.

Jared has his back to me. He's staring out the window. The blinds are no longer pulled, and the moon hangs low in the darkened sky.

"Do you want a drink?" Evelyn asks, already holding the glass.

I shake my head.

"Why don't we get a coffee?" Carl suggests.

"I don't want a coffee," Evelyn fires back.

Carl clears his throat, and he and Evelyn have a silent conversation with their eyes.

"Coffee sounds lovely," Evelyn says stiffly. "Jared, will you stay with Layla?"

Jared looks away from the window. "Of course. Take all the time you want."

Evelyn and Carl leave, and once the door closes, I'm expecting Jared to speak. He doesn't. He puts his hands in the pockets of his dark jeans.

"You don't have to stay, if you don't want to." My voice holds the note of bitterness I feel at his distance.

"I want to." Jared takes his hands out of his pockets and pulls up a chair beside the bed. He's not close enough for me to reach him.

"The Gardaí came to question me."

Jared finally looks at me. "What did you say?"

"What aren't you telling me?" I try to sit up higher, but the burn in my shoulder stops me. I hiss.

"Be careful. You'll hurt yourself." Jared moves, and his scent circles me as he helps me. His large hands grip my waist, the heat searing my skin. I lean forward, wanting to make him look at me, and when he glances down, my heart beats faster in my chest.

"I remember the lights going out," I whisper. I lick my lips. Jared doesn't move. His hands dig a little more into my hips, and I like how close he is. I feel safe. I feel secure. "That's it. Then the noise of the gun being fired."

Jared's eyes flutter closed before he releases me. "They're looking for the suspect." He sits back down, and I miss him already. I place my hands in my lap.

"I want you to stay with me." His request surprises me. He looks like he'd rather never see me again. Talk about mixed signals.

"Why?"

"To keep you safe."

"Didn't the shooting happen at your house?"

He works a muscle in his jaw. "I have added extra security."

As much as I would love the idea of being with Jared every second of the day, it isn't logical. "That robber isn't going to come after me, Jared."

"I still want you to stay with me."

He leans a little closer. The movement is subtle, but I sense him all the way down to my toes.

"No."

"It's not a request, Layla."

"Evelyn and Carl would never allow it. You're being paranoid. Like you said, it was a robbery," I reinforce.

"Evelyn and Carl won't be a problem." He sounds so sure, and I don't like it.

"They won't allow it, and they won't be bullied, Jared." My voice hitches as my heart pounds in my chest.

Jared inhales heavily. "Don't work yourself up," he grits between his teeth. Like this is my fault.

"Then stop being overbearing."

His grin is quick and unexpected. All the worry erodes away, one layer at a time.

"Overbearing?" His voice is light for the first time since I woke up, and I take full advantage of it.

"Yes, overbearing." I relax a little into the pillows. "Can we not fight? I just woke up from a coma," I remind him.

Brown eyes flash with guilt, and that wasn't my intention. I just want him to relax. Jared nods. "A truce for now."

I don't like the 'for now' part, but I take it.

"Tell me what I missed." I snuggle in deeper into the pillows and relish in Jared's deep voice as he tells me about all the visitors I've had.

I smile on and off before drifting into another peaceful sleep. When I wake, I'm alone and the room is in partial darkness. Images flicker across the television screen. I look to where Jared was seated and disappointment twists my stomach. That is, until I look beyond the chair and see a figure asleep on the couch.

"Jared." I say his name softly.

His reaction is immediate. He's standing and looking around him, his face tense.

"Jared."

His gaze lands on me, but he's still tense.

"You fell asleep."

He moves toward my bed. "How are you feeling?" he asks while running his hand across his face.

"I'm okay."

"You'd say that even if you weren't." His words aren't accompanied by a smile. He's still tense, even as he drags the chair closer to my bed. He's just sat down when a knock sounds at the door.

Jared gets up and answers it. I don't want anyone else to come into the room. Jared bends down and picks something up off the ground.

"Who is it?" I ask.

He glances at me over his shoulder while trying to hide what he's holding in his hand. A black wreath.

I'm about to ask who died, but he's racing from the room like a man possessed.

CHAPTER THREE

JARED

I'M STARING AT THE wreath in my hands. A small note has been attached.

RIP Layla.

I pull off the note before racing from the room. The hallways are pretty much empty. Three people approach, and one by one, I stop them.

I block the pathway of the first man. He tries to step around me, but I don't allow the movement as I pull down his collar, checking his neck for tattoos.

"What are you doing? Get off me!" The man fixes his shirt back in place after I release him.

I keep walking until I reach the reception desk.

"Who was just at Layla Masters's door?"

The receptionist frowns, and I slam the wreath on the counter.

She jumps slightly, her hand fluttering to her chest. "I didn't see anyone."

I spot three cameras. "I want to see the footage."

"I'm sorry, but I can't authorize that."

"Who can?"

She picks up the phone while I survey the area.

***

The videotapes show a man with a blue cap pulled low over his eyes. He drops the wreath, knocks on Layla's door, and takes off. There's no way of identifying who he is. The Gardaí take the wreath. I wish I had thought about my actions before the receptionist alerted them.

"It could be a prank," one of the Gardaí tells Evelyn, who's beside herself. "A jealous kid at school." I leave her and Carl in the hallway and spend my time helping Layla get everything packed up. Today she's going home. I'm beyond pissed that she isn't coming with me.

"You really should stay with me," I try again.

She's dressed in jeans and a T-shirt, her arm in a sling. She smiles at me and takes a tentative step forward. She taps her chin as if in thought, and I wait patiently, hoping she says yes. One word, and I'd have her out of here in seconds and secure in my home.

"No."

Disappointment turns to annoyance, which I try to hide. She brushes a lock of hair over her shoulder, and color blossoms on her cheeks. She's self-conscious as I watch her. I clear the distance between us and love when she looks up at me with her lips parted and eyes wide.

"You aren't making this easy." I reach out and touch her face.

"You wouldn't want me in your home. I snore."

I hold her face in my hands. "I said my home. I never mentioned my bed."

Her face burns red, and my cock gets hard.

"I snore loudly," she continues. "The sound travels through walls."

I love how flustered she is. "You don't snore. In fact, you barely move." How many nights have I watched her sleep here in the hospital?

She frowns. "How would you know that?"

"I know a lot about you, Layla." I dip my head to capture her mouth, when the door opens. I don't release her face. She's mine and I won't be rushed. I'd kiss her, only she's trying to look at the door. I slowly take my hands off her face, but I don't move away.

"Are you ready, sweetheart?" Evelyn asks, and Carl steps into the room. He picks up Layla's bags. I don't like this one bit, her staying with them. But I have several men stationed around her house. I won't rest until I find Chester and put a bullet into his head.

"I'll drive Layla to the house," I say.

"There's no need. Carl has the car ready." Evelyn smiles sweetly at me.

"I insist."

Her smile falters as her eyes narrow.

"That would be great, Jared," Carl, ever the diplomat, intervenes.

I hold out my hand for Layla. She flashes a glance at Evelyn before taking it.

"We'll be right behind you." Evelyn sings her reassurance, but I think it's more for me not to veer off with Layla.

As we leave the hospital, I keep checking all around us. My own security is positioned around the area. When they see me, they leave their stations and get into their vehicles. Layla slides into the passenger side of the car, and once I'm in, she struggles with buckling her belt.

I take my time reaching across her and clipping the belt closed.

"You seem tense," she tells me.

I sit back. "You do that to me." I grin.

Her cheeks heat. "Jared, be straight with me. Is this about the wreath? Because the Gardaí said it was most likely a prank."

I relax my shoulders. "Yeah, it's been on my mind." I start the car and pull out of the parking space. The Jeep with my security inside follows close behind me.

"I mean, it wasn't funny, but don't let it get to you."

I nod. "Okay."

"Why don't I believe you?"

I glance at Layla. She's observing me, her pouty mouth begging to be kissed. "I want to kiss you."

"You can't start saying that just because you want to change the topic."

"It's the truth."

She shifts, but I see a ghost of a smile.

"Do you not believe me?" I ask and slow down, pulling into a rest stop off the road. The Jeep pulls in behind us, but Layla doesn't seem to notice. She's too focused on me.

"What are you doing?"

Her breaths come out fast. I unbuckle my belt and move closer to her. Taking her face in my hands, I glance at her lips before I press mine against hers. She melts into me, and I hungrily take what is mine. Her mouth is warm and soft, and I run my tongue along her lips before breaking the kiss.

"I want you to stay with me," I try again.

Her laughter washes across my face. "You aren't going to give up?"

I run my thumbs across her cheeks. "Never."

She smiles, but it dwindles away. "I can't, Jared."

"For now," I answer. I'm patient.

After releasing her face, I pull us out of the parking space and get back on the road. I have to talk myself out of driving to my house and just forcing her inside. It takes a lot of restraint to take her home. Evelyn is standing beside the front door. Jesus fucking Christ, she's starting to wear on me.

"Will you come in?" Layla sounds unsure.

"No."

The disappointment flashes in her blue eyes.

I unbuckle my seat belt and reach across before unbuckling her too. "But I'll come by later."

She smiles. "That would be great."

"You can show me your bedroom."

Her face lights up like I knew it would, and I steal a quick kiss.

Her gaze darts to the house, where I know Evelyn is watching, before returning to me. "I doubt that."

I grin before releasing her from my stare. I slide out of the car and walk around to the passenger side door and open it for her. Evelyn makes her way toward my car.

"I got it," I tell her.

She reaches in to help Layla.

"I said I got it." I take Layla's arm and help her out. I let my fingers trail down her skin, and I'm tempted to push her back into the car.

"Welcome home, sweetheart." Evelyn leans in, and Layla breaks away from me and accepts the hug from Evelyn.

I close the passenger door. "I'll be back later," I say.

"No need. You've done enough."

I smile at Evelyn's condescending tone. "I insist."

Layla gives me a small wave as I get back into my car. I don't want to leave her, but once she's inside, I pull away from her house. The Jeep follows me closely, while my other security salutes me as I drive past their parked car and make my way home.

***

I arrive home, and the moment I open the door, Alex smiles at me. "What do you want?" I ask her.

"I wanted to make sure you were okay. You weren't answering my calls."

I don't go upstairs. I haven't since Layla was shot. "I'm fine." I make my way to my new quarters.

Alex follows me. "How is Layla?"

I stop walking and turn on her. "You don't give two fucks about Layla. Let's not pretend."

Alex tries to look shocked, but when I don't give her a reaction, she drops the act.

"I care about you." She folds her arms across her chest. The red V-neck jumper reveals just how large her breasts are, which I know is intentional. "You care about Layla. So I care."

I resume walking. "She's out of the hospital."

Alex's heels click noisily on the marble floor as she follows closely behind. "I'm so happy to hear it."

I snort at her lie. My bedroom is in darkness. I open the large, heavy green drapes.

"Look, I just want to support you, Jared. Like you did for me."

I haven't seen Alex since Mark's party. I don't want to have this conversation with her, so I pick the easy way to end it. "Thanks. But I'm good."

She's picking up my clothes off the floor, and God love her as she attempts to fold them. They end up being rolled into balls.

"You are folding creases in my clothes."

Her mouth forms a thin line. "Fuck's sake, Jay. I'm trying to help."

She's likely never folded a piece of laundry in her life, and I know her intentions are good. I run my hands down my face and sit on the edge of my bed. A part of me wants to let out all the fear that I'm drowning in.

"I'm tired."

Alex still holds one of my shirts as she sits down beside me on the bed. "You haven't been home. Were you staying at the hospital?"

"Yes."

"Your dad is worried." Alex rests a manicured hand on my thigh.

I remove it and get up off the bed. "I'm home now."

Alex wears a look of hurt before she recovers and stands up too. "Good. It will be great to get back to normal. Especially with the school dance coming up."

"I have to be somewhere soon. So..."

Alex forces a smile. She's really trying. "I'll come by later."

I'm ready to tell her I won't be here. "Great."

Her smile picks up. "See you then."

No, you won't.

She leaves me, and I ring my PI to see if there's any news on Chester. None. He hasn't been seen since the shooting.

"Call me if you hear anything," I say.

"I will."

I hang up and leave my room while I text Warren.

Are you around? I was thinking of catching up.

I send the text and make my way to the kitchen. Muffled voices have me stalling before I enter. My father and the head Gardaí are in the kitchen.

"Son, I didn't know you were up." My father walks toward me, directing me to the man beside him. "This is Inspector Reilly. He's been assigned to the robbery case."

Inspector Reilly places his coffee on the table before reaching out his hand. "Pleasure, Jay."

I shake his hand. He's freshly shaven, with two knicks along his jawline.

"I'm just going over the case notes, trying to figure out the entry point."

I release his hand, and my father sits down, but I don't join them. My phone dings and I take it out. Warren has agreed to meet me. *At least something is going right.*

"I have no idea. I didn't even hear him come up the stairs," I offer up.

Inspector Reilly helps himself to another biscuit. His gut begs him not to, but he shoves it into his mouth. I meet my father's gaze and wonder if he handpicked Inspector Gadget here.

"The good news is that we have word out to all art buyers about your stolen pictures."

Stolen pictures. This is news to me.

"Good," my father interjects. "They are highly valuable."

What is he doing?

Inspector Reilly opens a brown folder on the table. Crumbs fall onto the page, and he wipes them away. His nails are bitten down to stubs. I have zero confidence in his ability to do his job. He's sloppy. That has to be the reason he's here investigating a false robbery.

"Is William available? I just want to run through the details with him one more time. Make sure we haven't missed anything."

"Unfortunately, he is not. But I have spoken to William, and I can answer any questions." Father takes a drink of coffee.

The Inspector tuts. "It needs to be him."

"I am at your disposal, Inspector Reilly." My father smiles, and I want to know what the fuck he's doing.

"It's only between us." He smiles, and I want this cowboy out of my home.

"After the gun fired..." My father glances at me like mentioning a gun will set me off. I fold my arms across my chest, and when I don't flip out, he continues. "William went to go upstairs when he heard a noise down the hall. He arrived to find two pictures missing, and a man dressed in black slipping out the window."

"Once we find one of them, we'll get the other." The inspector closes his file and stands. "Thanks for the coffee. I better get to work."

"Yeah, you better," I say.

His smile falters as he looks at me.

"My son is eager to find the people who nearly killed him." My father is trying to cover up my hostility.

I stay in the kitchen as he escorts Inspector Reilly out. I don't give him a second when he steps back in.

"What are you doing? He isn't a real inspector."

My father isn't fazed. "He's investigating a robbery. You said there was a robbery."

I grit my teeth. "You didn't have to stage one."

His features twist with anger. "That's exactly what I had to do. But when you decide to tell me the truth, we can end this ruse."

"You dragged William into this?" I'm shaking my head.

"You left me no choice, son. A robber that takes nothing?" He raises a brow. "Even Inspector Reilly would figure that one out."

I refold my arms across my chest. "What exactly have you figured out?"

"This wasn't about you. It was about her. She dragged you into this mess," he says.

"I can't even mention her name without you getting defensive," he adds. "I bet he was a jealous ex of hers. God only knows what kind of people she hangs out with."

I take a step toward my father, and surprise lights up his eyes. I tell myself not to do something I might regret. "The gun was pointed at me. The bullet was meant for me, not her. No one knew she was here. So you're wrong."

My father doesn't look convinced. "Then tell me, son. Tell me what's going on." He closes the space between us. "Let me help you."

He wouldn't be able to do any more than I could with finding Chester, and I wouldn't implicate him in this. The fact that he and William staged a robbery is enough.

I have a meeting with Warren, and I hope it will put an end to Chester for good.

CHAPTER FOUR

LAYLA

I'm counting down the hours until Jared arrives. In the meantime, Evelyn doesn't leave my side. Flowers arrive from Jared, and Evelyn's tight smile tells me she isn't happy. Her behavior toward Jared feels heavy on my heart. Two of the most important people in my life don't seem to like each other.

Their animosity is becoming tiresome.

The television is on, but I don't believe that either of us is watching. "I want you to get along with Jared," I say while muting the volume.

"I do."

I don't respond.

Evelyn shifts on the large armchair, keeping her legs together, and veers toward me. "It's hard, Layla. He's a lot."

I nod. "I know. He's a lot in a good way."

She doesn't answer immediately. "He watches you so much." She frowns. "It's unsettling."

"Jared can be intense. But when you get to know him, you'll really like him."

Evelyn gets off the chair and joins me on the couch. "I don't doubt that, sweetheart. It's not about how he is with me. It's..." She's careful with her words. "It's how he is with you." She pauses again. "How you both are around each other."

I have no idea what she means. Evelyn takes my hands. "When you're with each other, it's like nothing else exists."

Embarrassment fills me right up to my bursting point. She's right. But that isn't a bad thing. "We haven't seen each other in such a long time. I think we just got caught up." I do my best to try to explain it.

"It's heavier than that."

I take my hands out of Evelyn's, not sure what she's implying.

"It's unhealthy," she finally says with a nod, like she's found the perfect word for what she's trying to explain.

My heart crashes, and pain uncurls its tight fist in my chest. I'm about to wrap my arms around my waist, but the sling restricts the movement. I can't keep looking at Evelyn.

"I'm sorry, sweetheart. I don't want to upset you. That's not my intention."

I can see the internal battle in her eyes.

"It's hard to explain, but I know what Jared and I have isn't unhealthy." When I say the words, I hate the fluttering that starts in my stomach.

Is it unhealthy? The way he beat Kieran nearly to death over a kiss, or the way he wants me to live with him? No, we know each other on a level that most don't. No one will ever understand what we have between us.

"Okay. I'm sorry." Evelyn pats my leg as the doorbell rings. The transformation is so obvious as she rises to open the door. She's shaking off our conversation with each step. Yet each step she takes away from me makes me feel sick.

Jared and I aren't unhealthy, I say again in my head. We saw the worst of each other. He saw me when I was vulnerable and broken. When everything was taken from me and I felt so destroyed, Jared would be there to piece me back together. That's not unhealthy, that's love.

So why do I feel sick at Evelyn's words?

"I'd love to know what you're thinking."

Jared fills the doorway. How can he continue to get better looking? Yet, he does.

"I'm thinking about you."

He steps into the room, and his grin makes my own lips rise. "I'm glad to hear it."

"It could be a terrible thought." I'm trying to fight the smile that wants to take over. He sits on the couch, leaving only a foot between us. A foot is too much.

"At least you're thinking about me."

I laugh. "How could I not?"

Jared takes my hand, and the look in his gaze makes me feel exposed. Like he can see past the smiles and laughter. Like he can see the agony that twists me up sometimes.

"What are we?" I ask.

"Jared and Layla," he says simply.

It's not the answer I want. Maybe he sees the disappointment on my face before I dip my head.

His fingers touch my chin, making me look at him. "We can be whatever you want us to be."

His finger taps my jaw as he waits for an answer. I notice Evelyn standing in the doorway and immediately take Jared's hand off my face. He doesn't react. I'm sure he's aware we aren't alone, but he pretends like it's still just us as Evelyn enters the room and sits down. Is this what she meant about Jared?

"Evelyn is making a stew for dinner. She's the best cook," I find myself saying.

Jared's eyes sparkle with amusement, but that smile doesn't grace his lips as he turns to Evelyn. "I can't wait."

She forces her lips to rise. "Great. We're very grateful to you, Jared, for staying with Layla at the hospital."

Jared stiffens beside me. "I wouldn't have it any other way."

"I know this isn't the best time, but I've spoken with Carl and we're covering the hospital bills."

Jared waves her off. "That's not necessary."

"We are her parents."

My face blazes. Talking about money makes me uncomfortable. Maybe growing up with nothing does that to a person.

"I'm grateful you would offer, Evelyn," he continues, "but it's already being taken care of."

"You had no right." Evelyn stands, and I'm shocked at the level of anger in her stance. She's not an angry person.

"You didn't have to do that, Jared," I agree with Evelyn. He shouldn't have paid my hospital bills. "It's not your responsibility." It isn't Evelyn's and Carl's either. I need to get a part-time job when I heal and pay Jared back.

"Or yours," I say to Evelyn before she can gloat.

"Yes, it is Layla." Evelyn's eyes widen.

"I'll get a job," I start.

Both Jared and Evelyn say, "No" in unison.

I get up off the couch. "At least you both agree on something."

"Where are you going?" Evelyn asks as I move past her.

"To the bathroom. Is that okay?" I hate biting at her, but she's not making this easy. I spend a little longer in the bathroom than necessary. A soft knock has me glaring at the door. I haven't locked it, and the handle rattles before the door opens.

I'm sitting on the edge of the bathtub. He leans against the frame and tilts his head to the side. "I had a chat with Evelyn."

I'm ready to tell him to get out.

His smirk makes me stop. "We've agreed to do better."

Surprise flitters through me, but I don't say anything.

Jared pushes off the doorframe. "I apologize for overstepping."

I nod. "Good."

"I also apologized for snapping." Evelyn's voice comes from behind the door.

I get up from the tub. "I don't want my favorite people in the world fighting," I say.

Jared doesn't smile but nods. Evelyn appears, and Jared steps aside so she can see in.

"We won't. Let's eat." Evelyn smiles, and I leave the bathroom with her.

We eat dinner, the conversation flowing steadily. Evelyn and Jared are still uptight with each other, but I don't expect things to change quickly. The fact they've acknowledged the hostility between them makes me happy.

After food, I'm hoping to have some time with Jared, but that doesn't look like it's in the cards.

"I'm going to have to cut this short," he tells me. "My father needs my help with some business jargon."

Evelyn looks way too happy. "That's a shame." She picks up his plate and takes them to get washed.

Jared smirks at her. "I know you'll miss me, Evelyn." He's teasing, and that makes me happy.

Evelyn seems surprised as she returns to get my plate. She raises a brow. "Drive safely," she tells him as she returns to the plates.

I get up to walk Jared out, but he holds up his hand. "Stay. I'll call you later." He walks around to me, and he's so confident as he bends down and takes my face in his hand. "Try to rest," he says before pressing a featherlight kiss to my lips.

I bob my head as he releases my face and leaves. I sit as Evelyn washes the plates. The noise is soothing, and all of a sudden, I do feel tired.

I get up from the table. "I think I'll go lie down."

"Do you need a hand getting upstairs?" Evelyn asks from the sink.

"No, thanks. I'm fine."

"Okay, sweetheart. Sleep well."

"Thanks." It's awkward with one arm, but I manage to drag the curtains closed, not before I spot a car outside the house. A man sits in the driver's side, his head bent as he looks at something in his lap. Fear has me watching him, but I dismiss my paranoia as an effect of Jared. He's so cagey, and I think it's rubbing off on me.

I lie on the top of the duvet. I didn't think I would really fall asleep, but I do.

Everything in the bathroom drips with gold. The chandelier is a ridiculous size. Each small teardrop crystal sparkles, and the reflection dances along the cream tiles. I step up to the double sinks. I press my index finger to one of the gold taps, and when I remove my hand, my imprint is left. As I move to grab some tissue to clean off my fingerprint, the lights go out. The room is pitch black, and I feel my way along the wall to the door.

I enter the hallway that has some light. I pause when I hear voices.

I can't make out the words or who Jared is speaking to. I walk in the direction of their voices.

"Jared." He has his back to me, and when he turns, the light from the window catches his features.

"Go back," he snarls.

Trepidation drips slowly down my spine as I look past Jared and to the other person, who I can't fully make out.

"The lights went out," I say when I reach Jared, wondering what's going on. I get a clearer view of the man in front of me. Jared's hand clamps down on my wrist. The impact startles me.

"The little bitch," Chester says, and that's when I follow his raised hand to the gun he's pointing at me. I'm ready to run when the world is ripped apart, and all I feel is pain.

Sweat coats me, and my shoulder throbs with a new kind of pain. It's like the wound is remembering again. My heart won't slow, and I sit up on the edge of the bed.

Chester shot me.

Chester was in Jared's home.

Chester shot me.

My heart palpitates as my brain decides to keep playing the last few seconds on a loop. I'm standing, trying to make the memory stop. Nothing makes sense.

Why did Jared lie? They'd been talking before I arrived...

My brain feels fuzzy. I shiver as the sweat dries on my skin. Reaching out, I pick up my phone. I've been sleeping for a few hours, and Jared has sent a few messages. I open his first message.

How are you?

His second message.

I hope your silence means you are sleeping

His third message has me sitting up.

I'll be back shortly.

I respond quickly.

I fell asleep. Can you leave coming over for tonight? I'm very tired.

I need time to figure out why Jared would lie. Why he lied to me, to his father, to Evelyn and Carl, and to the Gardaí. Was the wreath from Chester? Is that why Jared wanted me to stay with him? Disappointment continues to grow until it's all consuming.

My phone flashes with Jared's name. I hit the red button, cutting him off. Getting up, I enter the bathroom. Washing my face is a task with one arm, but I manage to freshen up. When I return, I have three missed calls from him.

I don't know what prompts me, but I make my way to the window. The car that was parked there before I went to sleep is still there.

Jared's name flashes up on my screen again. I swipe 'answer.'

"Why are you ignoring my calls?"

"Why is there a car parked outside my house?" I ask while clutching the curtain.

"What kind of car?" Jared is driving.

"Is this you, Jared?" I want him to say no. I want to be wrong about everything. But my doubt continues to grow.

"What kind of car?" He's angry.

"A black Audi."

He lets out a whoosh of air. "I'm on my way."

"I already told you not tonight. I'm tired." Guilt churns in my stomach, which makes no sense. I have every right to be mad at him.

"I won't keep you up." My guilt dissolves quickly at how easily he ignores my requests.

"I remember, Jared," I finally say and release the curtain. "I remember what happened."

He hasn't spoken, but he's still there. I can hear the hum of his car and the sound of his breathing.

"I remember being in your house."

"I'm on my way," Jared repeats.

"Am I a target?" I ask as fear clutches my throat. "Is that what the wreath was about?" All my fears come gushing out. "Will he come back and finish me off? That's why you're being so protective."

"Layla. I'm nearly there. Just stay calm. Where are you in your house?"

I wipe falling tears. "What does it matter?"

"Just tell me."

"I'm in my bedroom."

"Describe it to me."

I want to hang up on Jared, but another part of me doesn't want to be alone. "I have a double bed. The quilt has a purple flower pattern. I have a bedside table on either side. Jared, why did you hide this?"

"Do you remember the song about the fish?"

My eyes burn because I remember every single detail about myself and Jared. Every memory with him stands out, and Evelyn's words repeat in my head. *It's unhealthy.*

"Do you think we're unhealthy?" I ask, closing my eyes. Tears trickle down my face. Confusion with everything has me wanting to run.

"I think you're perfect."

I open my eyes at his words. He isn't driving anymore. I walk back to the window and pull open the curtains. His car is parked behind the Audi. He knocks on the window, and he says a few words to the man in the car before turning to the house. Our gazes clash.

Worry tightens his eyes, but he tries to cover it up with a smile as he holds up his pinky finger. "Remember the fish bit off this wee finger." He wiggles it like a worm, I can't see the action clearly from here, but from memory, I know what he is doing. This used to make me laugh, but I don't feel like laughing right now.

"I'll let you in." I hang up and make my way down the stairs, quickly hoping Evelyn doesn't hear us. I don't say anything as I open the front door. I place my finger over my lips so he's quiet as he follows me up the stairs. We need somewhere private to speak.

Once Jared is in my bedroom, I close the door and turn to him.

"I want an explanation now." My undamaged hand goes to my hip. Jared appears larger than life as he takes up all the space and air in my room. I try not to think of the fact that he's in my bedroom.

He nods. "Okay."

CHAPTER FIVE

JARED

“WHAT DO YOU REMEMBER?” I don't want to say more than I have to as I sit down on her bed.

Layla's hand leaves her hip, and she marches over to me. "No. That's not how this is going to work. Tell me why Chester shot me!" she whisper-shouts, and I reach out to touch her, but she moves aside, out of my reach.

"He was there for me. The bullet was meant for me." The truth stings worse when I say the words out loud. Layla getting shot was my fault.

Layla jolts back until she leans against the wall. Her lip wobbles, and she nibbles the pink flesh. "Jesus Christ, Jared. Why? Why would he want to kill you?"

"We had a fight, and it was retaliation."

She's shaking her head. "A fight? About what? Did you threaten him? His family? People fight all the time. I mean, I don't understand why you didn't tell the Gardaí that it was Chester. Now he's still running around out there with a gun." Layla's voice is tinged with hysteria.

I get up from the bed and advance toward her. She holds up her hand for me to stop, but I ignore her and gently pull her into my arms.

"The fight isn't important, Layla. I didn't think this would happen." I press a kiss to the crown of her head and she shoves me away.

"It doesn't make sense. Why are you hiding this?"

"Because I went to Chester to buy a gun. So if he's arrested and starts talking, I don't think it will work out well for me."

Layla blinks in rapid succession. "A gun?"

"Yes." I hadn't intended to share that fact with her.

"For what? Or should I say, who?" Her complexion pales, and when she makes her way to the bed and sits down, I don't stop her.

I'm close to the wall, and I stay put as I face her. "That doesn't matter."

She's shaking her head. "Please stop saying it doesn't matter. Just fucking tell me."

I shouldn't tell her. No good can come from sharing the truth. Yet, I find myself opening my mouth and letting it out. "For Bert."

Layla presses her hand to her lips, and a loud sob erupts. "Oh, Jared."

She stays like that for a while, and I have no idea how to comfort her.

"You got a gun to kill Bert?" she asks.

I nod in acknowledgment.

She cries again. "You were going to take a life?"

My fury spikes. "Fuck's sake, Layla. It's not a life. He doesn't *deserve* to live."

She's shaking her head. "You were going to take a life, Jared."

I'm kneeling in front of her. "Keep your voice down."

I reach up and brush her face, attempting to erase her falling tears, but she jerks out of my grasp. The look of revulsion I see in her stunning gaze forces me to stand.

"You need to pack a few belongings. I can't protect you here."

She sniffles. "What? You want to take me to your home, where I got shot?"

I grind my teeth. "It's the safest place right now. I have plenty of security."

"I already said no."

"This time, I'm not asking."

She stands up. I've pushed too hard, but I'm sick of playing nice with Layla. It's been too long of her staying here and me having to deal with fucking Evelyn.

Layla clears the space between us, and her hand smacks into the center of my chest. The impact is minimal. "No. You can't boss me around."

"You're still a target."

"I'm not going." She hits me again, a bit harder this time.

"Evelyn and Carl will be targets too."

Her lips part, and indecision filters slowly into her features. "Don't try to manipulate me."

"I'm telling you the facts. If you come with me, I'll send word out so Chester knows not to target your home. I'll leave some security here."

Layla turns away from me. "Get the word out? Are you part of his gang?" She waves off the question. "Just say I'm living with you. Won't that be enough?"

"No, it's not enough. Someone might see you here." I'm clutching at fucking paper straws that have spent too much time in water, but she doesn't know that. Having her with me is all I want.

Her gaze wavers, and she's about to respond when the door opens.

Evelyn appears. "I'd like the door kept open."

I can't even glance at her. Layla is nineteen, not nine. But out of respect for Layla, I say nothing about Evelyn's intrusion.

"Yeah. No problem," Layla says.

Evelyn steps into the room. "Are you okay?" she asks Layla.

Layla looks at me before forcing a smile onto her face. "Yeah, yeah. Just talking."

Evelyn taps her foot on the floor several times. "I'm only downstairs." Her tone is sharp.

What the fuck did she think I was doing? I finally glance in the direction of Evelyn and find her watching me.

"Okay," Layla says and Evelyn leaves.

"What the hell do I tell them?" Layla whispers.

"I can do it," I offer. I won't be gentle either. My intentions coming over here were to carry her down the stairs and into my car.

Layla glares at me. "Wouldn't you love that?"

I'd smile at how beautiful she looks when she's pissed, but this isn't the time.

"Why don't we tell them the truth?" Layla tries to negotiate.

"What will they do, Layla? They'll go to the Gardaí, and I might find myself in a lot of trouble."

She rubs her face. "How long will I have to leave?"

"Not long," I reply.

"Chester isn't just going to go away, Jared." Layla intakes a large gulp of air. "What do you intend to do? Shoot him too?" Layla's eyes widen. "Oh my God. When did this become okay?" She's hyperventilating.

I go to her and take her face. "Take a deep breath."

She's trying to push me away. I've given in to her tantrums before, but this time, I keep my hold on her face and speak with more force. "Take a deep breath, Layla."

She does.

"No one is going to die."

"You swear?" Her sharp intakes and loud exhales are what I concentrate on.

"If Chester were shot, they would blame me. I'm not stupid. As much as I want him dead, I won't be shooting anyone."

Layla's eyes water. "Promise me, Jared." Her lip drags down.

I lean my forehead against hers. "I promise." I press a kiss to her lips. "Pack a few things. We can always come back for more."

"What do I say to Carl and Evelyn?" Panic widens her eyes.

"I can tell them. In a nice way," I suggest, and I would be nice for Layla, seeing she's in such a state.

She shakes her head. "I'll do it."

Her body deflates, and her shoulders drop.

I release her.

"This is for their protection," she says, as if trying to reinforce that lie.

I incline my head. "Theirs and yours." I don't give two fucks about them, but Layla does.

"I want you to wait in the car."

I take a step toward her. "No."

"Jared. Just give me a minute. Please."

I want to warn her not to keep me waiting, but the pleading in her voice has me clenching my jaw.

"I'll be in the car." I press a kiss to her forehead before leaving. Evelyn is at the bottom of the stairs.

"You're leaving?" she asks.

I smile. "Yes, I am."

That leaves her unsettled, and she marches up the stairs.

Outside, I get into my car. I have two missed calls from Alex.

I'm busy, I text her and look back at Layla's house.

I can't imagine the conversation is going well with Evelyn. It takes a lot of restraint not to get out of the car and rush into the house to get Layla.

Thirty painful minutes pass before Layla leaves the house with a small backpack. She won't meet my gaze as she climbs into the passenger side. The door closes, and with shaky hands, she struggles to put on her belt.

"Let me help you." I reach across to grab the belt.

"I got it."

I ignore her.

"Jared, stop." Her gaze meets mine, and she's beyond pissed.

"I'm trying to keep you safe."

She clips her belt into place. "You know when people say take off the band-aid quickly? That it's less painful?" She looks up at me. "It's not. I think I broke her heart."

Layla looks out the window, and after a few moments, she speaks quietly. "Just go."

Evelyn will recover, and Layla will be safe. That's all that matters to me. "I'll leave two of my men here to keep Evelyn and Carl safe," I offer up as I pull onto the road.

"Thank you."

"You're welcome." The drive to my home is silent, but the quiet is not uncomfortable. With Layla at my side, silence isn't a void I want to fill. I could sit with her like this forever.

The gates to my home open, and I drive up to the house. I'm sure my father is going to be ecstatic when he sees Layla.

"You will be safe here," I say when I unclip my belt.

Layla doesn't respond. She's working on her own seat belt and struggles to get the door open. By the time I get around to her side, she's still trying to get out. I could stand here to prove a point that she needs help. I open the door and pick her bag up off the floor while offering her my hand. She has to take it. She's still pissed, and it's not a look I've seen on Layla before.

"I'll show you to your room." I close the car door and Layla follows me into the house. She pauses at the stairs, and a new kind of fear enters her features.

"I won't let anything happen."

She resumes walking, and that fucking bothers me. She doesn't think I can keep her safe. I've always kept her safe.

"You would have been upset if I shot Bert?" I ask.

Layla stops walking and turns to me. "Of course." She frowns while wrapping one arm around her waist. "It's murder, Jared."

It would be justice. I don't voice my true motivation.

"If you had," she continued, "you would have gone to jail."

I nod. I knew that, and I had been fully prepared to do the time. I would have tried to stay out of jail, but it was a gamble I was willing to take if it meant bringing him to his fucking knees.

Layla unwraps her arm from her waist, and she's in front of me like a spitfire. Her hand hits my chest heavily. "What about me? You would have just left me? How could I have coped with that?"

Her breathing is growing harsh again, and she's struggling to keep focus. Her gaze darts everywhere as tears leave her eyes. "How could you give up your life? Have we not given enough of our time?"

She's in my arms, and her tears grow heavier, her sobs louder. This is where I'm meant to be. Right here protecting Layla.

"Everything is okay." I press a kiss to the crown of her head.

"No, Jared. It's not." She tries to wriggle from my hold.

I let her.

She wipes her eyes. "This is just all too much."

She'll get used to her life here. I continue walking, and she follows as I take her to the room I had prepared for her two weeks ago. The moment she ended up in the hospital, I knew I had to bring her here.

I open the door and let her step into her new room. I don't really intend to leave her in here for long. She'll be in my bed soon, but I have to show patience. She walks around the large space.

"Do you like it?" I ask.

She runs her hand along the white duvet. "It's lovely." Her voice is heavy.

I look back down the hall and notice William waiting for me. I place Layla's bag on the floor. "I'll let you get settled."

She doesn't look at me, but I see the nod of her head.

William waits as I close Layla's door, then he hands me a slip of paper. I want to tell him to just say what my father sent him to say, but I open the note instead. I'm surprised to see I have a visitor in the library. I look up at William, but he doesn't meet my eye, and he's getting ready to walk away.

"Who is it?"

He swallows. "Your mother, Master Jay."

CHAPTER SIX

LAYLA

I fold my hands in front of me, trying to find meaning in all of this. Jared's plan to kill Bert has dread chasing me. I look over my shoulder, expecting to see something large and dark looming. Instead, the bedroom door opens and three women file in.

They wear the same uniforms—navy trousers, a white shirt, and a navy jacket. The ladies have their hair pinned back so severely that it stretches the smiles on their faces.

"Miss Masters, we are here to serve." The taller of the three steps forward, and her lips curl back over her teeth. Thoughts of a horse spring to mind. It's not a fair analysis of her looks, but I can't stop the comparison.

"Serve me?" I'd laugh, only the dread I've been sensing hasn't left. My confusion keeps deepening.

"Yes..." She glances over her shoulder while sweeping her hand toward the other two ladies. "We are here for you."

Servants. I have servants.

"There's no need. I'm sure you have other things to do."

The lady's smile falters, and she clears her throat. "Please. Master Jay has assigned us to help you."

There's an awkward silence as they wait for me to say something. I've never had anyone serve me before. I need to talk to Jared about this. We weren't brought up with silver spoons in our mouths. More like cheap plastic ones.

Each lady waits expectantly. Maybe having them here will be a welcome distraction until I tell Jared how ridiculous all this is.

"Maybe we can start with your names."

"I'm Kerry." Kerry continues to smile, and I try to shake off the horse comparison, but it's impossible. Her smile is so wide that I can see her gums. Her black bangs are thick and rest just above her brows. The rest of her hair is pinned back neatly.

The second lady steps forward. Her brown hair is in a tight bun, and she has red, rosy cheeks. "I'm Andrea."

"And I'm Amanda." She's the smallest of the three, and the youngest. All her features are pixielike, but from the sharpness of her brown eyes, I don't think her size would have anyone underestimating her.

"I'm Layla." I look at each lady. They don't tell me they already know this, which I'm sure they do, but I want to even the playing field.

"I've never had anyone take care of me before." The awkwardness returns, but Kerry gives a little clap of her hands.

"Let us take the lead, then."

My shoulders relax. "Thank you, Kerry."

The activity around the room is instant. Kerry gives instructions, and the ladies move. Amanda makes her way to the bathroom, while Andrea lights the fire. Kerry has picked up my bag, but I immediately reach for my only possession.

"I can do that."

She has so much gum on display. "Not at all. Allow me."

I don't want to be rude. "No, please." I hold out my hand, and she passes me the bag.

"I'll get some food," Kerry says.

I'm not hungry, but I don't stop her as she leaves the room. I sink onto the bed with the bag in my hand. I pull down the zipper and reach in, taking out Carl's sweater. This is the sweater I keep hidden from Carl and Evelyn. For so many nights, it gave me comfort as fear tried to keep me awake. I raise the garment to my nose and inhale the smell that still lingers in the fibers. The crackle of the fire has me opening my eyes.

Andrea has her back to me. The distant rumble of the bath filling has me getting up off the bed and walking over to the large antique chest of drawers. I don't bother with the top drawers but bend down and struggle to open the bottom one with one hand. I finally manage, and it's there I put Carl's sweater for safekeeping. I push the drawer back in with my foot, but I don't step away from the dresser as the conversation with Evelyn I had plays out in my mind.

"You're leaving?"

"Only for a few nights, Evelyn." I try to downplay the hurt that's blatant on her face.

"Is this because of me and Jared?"

"No. I just want to spend some time with him." I cling to the strap of my bag.

"I don't think this is a good idea, Layla." Evelyn's fretting. That's something I've never seen her do.

My lip trembles, and I bite the meaty flesh. "I need you to trust me."

Evelyn steps closer. "I do trust you. I just don't think going back to Jared's home is wise. I don't understand the sudden shift in your decision."

No words will make this right, I know that. The fact is, I have to leave. I need to keep Carl and Evelyn safe.

"I need space from you, Evelyn. I need time with Jared without you hovering over me." I can't stay any longer as I watch the woman who gave me a home crumble in front of me.

I turn away from her but pause at the kitchen door. "I love you, Evelyn. I'll call every day."

"I love you too."

I can't look back. The pain in her words propels my steps out the door.

"Miss Masters, your bath is ready."

I stiffen as Amanda appears beside me. I exhale loudly, trying to relax as I shake off the memory of Evelyn.

"I'll need you to help me with my clothes." I don't exactly want help, but I'm exhausted, and removing everything with one arm is something I don't look forward to doing.

Amanda helps me, being careful with my arm. Once I'm down to my underwear, I make my way into the bathroom alone. The steam has fogged up the mirror, like it knows I don't want to see my face. Guilt is choking me, and I don't need to see it in my gaze.

My underpants slide down easily, and I kick them off. Removing my bra with one hand is a problem, but one I manage to resolve. Once naked, I step into the bath. The heat encases me as I sink right under the water. I'm trying to outrun my thoughts, but they haunt me like a ghost, and I break the surface of the water. Raising both hands, my shoulder burns, and I reduce my movements but move my fingers around, allowing my hands to filter through all the bubbles.

Sounds come from my bedroom. The ladies are still there, waiting to serve me. I don't think I could ever get used to having people waiting on me hand and foot. I don't stay too long in the bath because I don't find the freedom I'm seeking from my thoughts.

A soft knock on the door has me calling out. "Yes."

"May I come in?" I think it's Amanda.

I glance down at my body, which is hidden under all the bubbles. "Yes."

It is Amanda who enters, with a white bathrobe and some towels. "For when you're ready to get out."

I sit up slightly. "I'm ready now." She places the towels on the vanity table and steps closer with the bathrobe, opening it.

She already helped me get undressed, so what does it matter if she offers me a little more help. I stand up quickly and get out of the bath. The robe is placed on my back, and I slip my arms into the sleeves before bringing the gown together with the large belt. When I turn, Amanda hands me a towel for my hair.

"Thank you."

"You are very welcome." She makes herself busy getting out a hair dryer as she uses it to dry the steam off the vanity mirror.

"It's okay." I don't need the mirror cleared. I don't want to see myself.

Amanda turns off the hair dryer before pulling out the small stool. "I'll do your hair."

I sit down. Amanda works on my hair, and I shift in the seat, wanting to get up. Darkness keeps creeping in, and if I move, I might be able to outrun the dread that won't leave me alone.

My hair is only half-done when I stand. "It's fine. I like it to dry naturally." The bathroom is too warm, and I don't wait for Amanda to reply before entering my bedroom. Fresh clothes are laid out on my bed; clothes I didn't bring. A pair of gray high-waisted trousers with wide legs are the first thing I reach for. The woolen material and the cut of them tell a story of their worth. The cream cashmere V-neck sweater is soft under my fingertips. The rattle of a tray has me looking at Kerry as she sets the silver set down on the table nestled close to the window.

"Some tea and sandwiches." She glances at me with a smile before taking everything off the tray and placing it neatly on the table.

Amanda arrives out of the bathroom. "Shall I help you dress?"

I want to say no, but her help will make the process quicker. I give her a nod of my head.

Andrea moves across the room and into the bathroom. Kerry leaves with an empty tray, and it's just me and Amanda.

"Have you worked for Jared long?" I ask. She frowns and I correct myself. "Jay."

"No. We were only recently hired by Master Jay."

I'm nearly dressed, and as perfect as this outfit feels, it also causes me concern. He had time to get these clothes, the right sizes, and have them placed in this room. Now, I have staff that he just all of a sudden hired?

"When did Jay hire you?" I ask.

Amanda looks over at the table where Kerry had been, and I wonder if she's searching for approval to speak. When she realizes it's just the two of us, she answers. "Two weeks ago."

My stomach tightens. "Thank you, Amanda."

Amanda helps me put my sling back on before gathering up the bathrobe. I sit at the small table, and it's not until I start to eat that I realize I'm pretty hungry.

Andrea finishes cleaning the bathroom, and Kerry returns. "Thank you, all. But I'm fine now."

Without question, Andrea and Amanda leave my bedroom, but Kerry lingers.

"Our sole purpose is to serve you, so one of us will be outside your door if you need."

My God, this is ridiculous. I really need to find Jared and speak to him about this.

"Thank you, Kerry."

Kerry leaves, and I push my food aside. I sit a few minutes, until the crackle of the fire drives me out of the chair. I grab a pair of white tennis shoes that take me a few minutes to get into before leaving the room. True to her word, Kerry is standing outside my room. She glances at me.

"I'm just taking a walk," I say, hoping she won't follow me. She doesn't.

The foyer is enormous, and I don't think I could ever not be amazed at the sheer size and décor of this mansion. The stairs come into view, and I pause. Jared's quarters are up here, and I'm sure that's exactly where I will find him. He placed me on the ground floor, so I didn't have to remember...

Each step I take is heavy. I'm tempted to turn around and wait in my room for Jared to come to me, but I keep pushing up the stairs. I don't want to be alone. I don't want to stand still. I don't want to feel this fear I can't shake off.

I reach the third floor, and the air is heavy. I'm not supposed to be up here. That's the feeling that tightens every bone in my body as I move mechanically across the landing. I stop at where I stood the night of the shooting. There isn't a blemish on the oak wooden floor. The smell of fresh paint and polish covers up the blood and fear of what took place.

"The little bitch." Chester's words send a shiver along my spine. I dip my head into my chest on reflex as I glance at the window where he stood. Light flitters across the floor, blinding the darkness of the moment.

I close my eyes and let the warmth of the sun caress me, but everything in me screams. I open my eyes as my vision wavers, and I want to cave in and curl up right here on the floor. There's something building inside me as I turn away from the window and the heat of the sun, stepping deeper into the space. I pause at Jared's bedroom door before entering; he isn't here. The bathroom I used the night of the shooting makes me pause as well. It's like standing on the edge of a platform, and there's a speeding train making its way toward me. I have no control as my foot lifts, and I step into the bathroom.

I run my tongue along my teeth as everything blurs. My strength evaporates as the burn in my shoulder erupts. Jared is safety. That's all I've ever known. I'm here in his home, and I've never felt so lost, so unsafe, so confused. I leave the bathroom, and I'm ready to give up my search when a door at the end of the hall catches my attention. I saw Jared look at it before while touching the key that hung around his neck.

Each step I take toward the door has my pain falling off me like a second skin. I can almost imagine the anguish sliding off me and leaving a trail behind. *Curiosity Killed the Cat.* Those words ring in my mind as I reach for the door and turn the handle.

CHAPTER SEVEN

JARED

I ENTER ONE OF the many sitting rooms. I refer to this room as the waiting room, because this is where most visitors are taken.

I try not to react as the woman who claims to be my mother stands. I don't like how I recognize myself in her dark eyes. The bow of her lips is a replica of mine. She's tall, especially for a woman. Her slight build doesn't make her look timid or tame. She holds herself with a fierceness that reminds me of a lioness.

"What do you want?" I ask.

She bristles. Her reaction is instant. "That's how you greet your mother?" Hurt flows quietly under her words; I can detect the pain.

"You claim to be my mother," I answer. It's obvious that she's my mother from her features alone, but I also remember her. She's older, but she is my mother.

She nods solemnly. "It's been a long time."

Did she expect me to feel sorry for her? She gave up on me.

"What do you want?" I ask again. I wave her off and close the door heavily behind me as I step deeper into the room. "Does Father know you're here?"

It would undo him, and I can't allow that. No matter how angry I am with him, he found me and gave me my life back. She, on the other hand, destroyed my life.

My mother's eyes widen, and panic has her gaze darting around the room. "No. I only wanted to speak to you."

I grin. "Are you sure I shouldn't get him? Let this be a family reunion." My grin melts off my face.

Her frantic eyes settle on me, and she wrings her hands in front of her. "I was trying to protect you."

I can't give her a second look as hatred burns through my veins, destroying the last of my control.

"Trying to protect me by taking me away from my father? By placing me in the home with those fucking monsters?" I'm in front of her. "Do you have any idea what they did to me?" I want to kill her.

My mother startles, her brows dragging down. "Monsters? What happened? Jared?" She reaches for me.

I step away and pull my control back, building the walls that will keep me sane and safe. "Why are you here, and why now?" I appreciate how controlled my voice is, and with that knowledge, I grow calmer.

"I put you in the foster system to protect you. I didn't think anything would happen. Did someone hurt you?" She reaches out to me again but wisely stops and places her hands behind her back. She gathers some of her emotions.

"This is your last chance, Maura. I've been here for seven years, so why are you here now?"

"Seven years?" She seems to stumble before seeking out the chair behind her. "He's had you here for seven years?" Her emotions level, and I think she's going to throw up. "I saw an article about a shooting in the house. When your name was mentioned, I realized he had found you." Her focus bounces around the room before she looks at me. "I was only trying to protect you."

I smirk, and I hope she feels the coldness down to her soul. "Well, you didn't."

Her throat bobbles as she swallows and nods. "All he wants is your money." Tears fall from her brown eyes. "He will do anything to have your money."

The door to the waiting room opens, and my father steps in. I'm walking toward him. I don't want him to have to deal with her. "I'll get rid of her," I tell him.

He closes the door like I haven't spoken. "Maura, I was wondering when you would make your reappearance."

There's no devastation in his voice. If anything, he sounds gleeful. When I look back at Maura, she's standing. Her chest rises and falls rapidly, and she reminds me of a drowning man. I'm okay watching her drown. In fact, I hope she does.

"Seven years, you've had my son." Each word is low, but it drives her feet toward him. I step in her way, blocking her. She halts and frowns.

"You have no idea what he's capable of." She's pointing around me, but my father's hand on my shoulder has me stepping aside.

"I think you should leave, Maura. You are upsetting Jay."

I don't have time to react as she slams her open palm across my father's face. "You changed my son's name." She's screaming, and I've fucking had enough. I grab her hand before she hits him again.

"Get out of our home. Neither of us ever wants to see you again."

My father backs me up. "You heard Jay. Leave."

I release my mother.

The door to the waiting room opens, and two security guards step into the room. I look at my father. I don't think that's necessary, but I don't stop them as they step toward my mother, who is growing frantic.

She's shaking her head as they take an arm each. "Jared, listen to me. He only wants the money."

I don't respond as they drag her from the room.

"He killed my husband." Her accusation is the last thing I hear as she's dragged from the room.

"How did she get in?" I ask.

"That is a question I'm asking myself." My father steps up to me and places a hand on my shoulder. "Are you okay, son?"

I nod. "She doesn't think you're her husband," I say. She's lost her mind. That fact should sadden me, but it doesn't.

"I'll make sure she never gets in here again," my father promises as he goes to leave the room. Instead, he turns to me.

"Are you okay?"

"Yes." I want to ask why I wouldn't be. She means nothing to me. But, the more I want to elaborate, the more silent I become.

My father takes my silence to mean I don't care. "I wanted to speak about our houseguest."

I tighten my fists, ready to defend Layla.

My father raises a hand, the large silver watch catching the light. It's the same watch from my memory. He drops his hand, and the watch disappears. "I understand that she's important to you, so I want to meet her."

"No," I say immediately. I won't let anyone hurt her.

"Jay, I just thought the three of us having dinner together would be nice. I want her to like me." His voice holds a note of vulnerability. A note I've never heard before.

I still don't want him near her.

"You have my word," he continues. "I will keep the conversation to civil matters."

I'm still not convinced.

My father stands straighter. "The weather and school."

"No mention of the shooting or her foster parents or how we grew up." I take a step closer to my father. "I won't allow one word to hurt her."

He nods. "I'm starting to understand that, son." He reaches out and squeezes my shoulder before leaving.

I go in search of Layla. She's not in her room. Kerry is outside her door and points at the stairs. "She took a walk, Master Jay."

I'm taking the steps two at a time. What is she thinking going up here?

I reach the third floor, and she's nowhere in sight. "Layla?" I call.

"Here."

I stop walking and return to the living space. She rises from the couch.

"What are you doing up here?" I ask.

"When Chester shot me, I don't remember what happened after he fired the gun." She sits up further, her blonde hair spilling over her shoulder. The *V* of her cream sweater shows off her generous cleavage. When I had selected the top, I knew it would be perfect on her.

"William rang an ambulance." I don't step into the living space.

"It's funny. I could have died, and everything, every single moment, would have ceased to exist for me. But for you, it would have gone on."

I scratch my forehead. Her thoughts are morbid. "Come back downstairs."

"Did you cry?" She gets up from the couch.

"No," I answer honestly.

Is that disappointment I see in her eyes? I grin. "Would you have wanted me to cry?"

She steps around the couch and walks over to me. She shrugs and lets out a half-hearted laugh. "I don't know."

"I mean, I'm sure I can cry if it makes you feel better." I narrow my eyes.

She laughs. "I was just curious."

I reach out my hand, and she takes it. "My father wants to officially meet you. We're going to have a meal together tonight."

She's looking up into my eyes with the fear of God in hers, and I pull her a little closer. "I swear to you, he only wants to meet you."

She swallows and nods. "Yeah, I can't wait."

I'm not sure if she's telling the truth, but I accept her words as truthful. I just want us back downstairs. We leave the living room, and Layla stops, looking behind her.

"The room at the end of the hall. What's in it?"

My gut twists. "Why?"

She shrugs as she glances up at me. "I was exploring, and it's the only locked door on this floor."

What would she think if she knew? I'm staring back at the door along with her. My gut twists again.

"It was once a servant's room. Now..." I meet Layla's gaze. "It's storage."

"Okay." She accepts my word. "Speaking of servants, I don't need any."

I take her hand in mine and start pulling her back down the stairs.

"That's no problem."

She narrows her eyes. "That easy?"

I grin. "I will dress you and undress you. You can't manage with one arm."

Her face burns, and I stop us at the top of the landing. "It's up to you, Layla. Either they serve you, or I do."

She's struggling with her answer, and it delights me. Will she pick me?

"Fine. Kerry and the girls stay."

I continue our descent down the stairs. "Good. I want you to be happy here." *Happy with me.*

Layla can't hold my stare. "I am," she lies. I accept her lie, as one day I know she will be happy with me.

"I took the liberty of buying you some dresses. I think the red one will be stunning on you tonight."

Layla doesn't speak until we reach the foyer. "It almost seems you've been planning this for a while."

"I have been." I have no need to lie. "Ever since you got injured, I've wanted you here with me, where I can keep you safe."

Layla reaches up and touches my face. "You don't have to keep protecting me." Pain radiates from her eyes.

I capture her hand in mine again. "I will always protect you, Layla."

No matter the cost.

CHAPTER EIGHT

LAYLA

"**C**OME ON." JARED APPEARS relaxed as he takes my hand in his. His smile showcases his dimples, and I can't stop the smile that grows on my own face.

My nerves seem to be jumping all over the place. Meeting Jared's father for the first time is daunting and yet exciting. Jared's dimples disappear, and he squeezes my hand as we walk through the foyer. I feel overdressed as the red material swishes a fraction of an inch above the marble floor. My hair is loose, and Amanda worked so carefully on my hair and makeup that when I looked in the mirror, I was surprised by what I saw. I've opted to leave my sling off so as not to ruin the stunning dress. I'm careful with the placement of my arm and keep it stiff along my side. Jared stops walking, and I'm surprised when he releases my hand and faces me.

"If for any reason you feel uncomfortable, just let me know."

His words make me unsure. A nerve tics in Jared's jaw.

"Why would I feel uncomfortable?" I ask.

I don't get an answer.

"Exactly, Layla" Jared's father appears in the hallway, and he's a formidable force. "That's the same question I would ask, too."

I don't expect his next action as he reaches me and carefully pulls me into a hug that drags a small, short squeal from me. My hands hang at my sides until the shock passes, and I hug him back. He smells of cologne and carries the coolness of fresh air; the cologne tickles my nose.

"So glad to have you in our home," he says, not letting me go as he holds me at arm's length.

"Alright, Father." Jared speaks from behind me.

Jared's father releases me, and I quickly glance at Jared and raise both brows. He had no need to worry. Straight away, his father is being nice. "Great to meet you too, Mr. McGivney."

"Athar. You can only call me Athar. Mr. McGivney makes me feel old."

I nod that I will as he steps aside to let both Jared and I walk in front of him. Surprise flitters through me as Jared takes my hand, and my head twists up to him. He isn't looking at me; instead, he is leading me down the hall and into the dining room.

The room is large, but I expected nothing less. The chaos of paintings, flowers, and furniture isn't what I expected, though, and it's the first room that seems like it's being used.

Both men allow me to take in the room. One side has photographs, and I take my hand out of Jared's and walk toward the large gilt edge frame. I want to know everything about him, and I focus on the images that hang on the walls. Jared steps up beside me, and even though the room is vast, it feels so small with him at my side. Emotionally, I can't concentrate, so focusing on the images gives me a moment before Jared's body heat burns my back. He reaches over my shoulder as he points at the picture I'm looking at. It's Jared holding a mic. The assembly in front of him holds hundreds of people, and they're caught up in whatever Jared is saying. The photo is black and white, and he looks breathtaking.

"A speech I had to make on responsibility."

I look over my shoulder at Jared and stare at his chest before slowly meeting his dark eyes. "Responsibility?" It sounds like a silly question.

"Yes, Layla. Don't seem so surprised." The laughter in Jared's voice has my lips rising. "Maybe one day you might address the school, too."

I blink a few times at his sentence. That sounds like a nightmare. I don't get to voice the horror I feel, but from the dimples that appear on Jared's cheeks, I see he already knows. A servant arrives, carrying a tray with steaming plates of food.

Athar is already seated at the head of the table, and Jared and I join him. I'm to Athar's left, and Jared is to his right. Sitting down, I exhale and then breathe in the scent of food that is lowered in front of me from a second servant. A third servant places Jared's food in front of him, and when I meet his gaze, he grins.

I can't stop staring at the fish that looks undercooked on my plate. A few leaves and shavings of vegetables are all that decorate the fish.

Jared laughs. "That's squid, in case you're wondering."

I pick up my knife and fork and have to really work on cutting off a piece. Stuffing it into my mouth, I give Jared a quick smile. "It's nice."

Chewing the fish takes a while. Surprisingly, the small shavings of vegetables are divine. We chat as we eat. Athar sticks close to the topics of school, the weather, and shockingly, gardening. Jared has shared that knowledge with him. He doesn't mention the foster home we grew up in or anything about the shooting that took place in his home. It makes the avoided topic hang heavy in the air.

The plates are removed and our drinks are replenished. Athar sits back in his chair.

I'm waiting for the conversation to move to what everyone is thinking, but it doesn't go there. Instead, Athar stands.

"I think I'll take my leave."

"It was lovely meeting you, Athar."

"You too, Layla." Athar smiles before giving Jared a nod of his head.

I take a peek at Jared, and he doesn't seem surprised at all by this. In fact, I'd say he appears relieved.

"Next time, I will cook for you," Jared says once his father has left.

"The fish was lovely," I lie. He laughs as I sink into the chair. "That sounds nice, you cooking," I add.

Jared rises. "You might regret saying that."

I doubt I will.

"Come on," he says, holding out his hand for me to take.

I take it and don't ask where we're going as he leads me out of the room. The staircase comes into view, but he doesn't veer over to it. Instead, Jared takes me down the hallway where my room is. My pulse spikes as he stops at the door beside mine. I'm surprised to see Kerry still stationed outside my room. I swallow words as Jared tugs on my hand.

"This is my room."

His room.

Jared keeps his fingers threaded through mine as we enter.

Jared's room is tidy, but that doesn't surprise me. It always was. A large queen-size bed is situated on a huge black shaggy rug. The moss green bedding drapes on either side of the bed. The furniture is antique, like the rest of the house. The wardrobe, nightstand, and dresser all match. Once again, I can't stop the thought that it's so far away from how we grew up.

Jared releases my hand and walks over to his bed. He sits down and observes me as I check out his room. My heels click on the dark wooden floor. The blank walls are freshly painted in a soft gray. Jared was always a fan of movie posters, and now I wonder what had happened to them. Did they remind him of before, or had he just outgrown that time of his life? It's moments like these that I realize we lost so much time with each other.

Casting my gaze back to Jared, my stomach flips. The way he's looking at me has me fidgeting with my hand. Jared gets up and goes to his wardrobe before returning with something grey. My heart leaps with recognition, and he pats the bed beside him.

Oh my God.

I gather the red material of my dress as I walk on shaky legs over to Jared. I sit down slowly, never taking my eyes off the sweater. My vision blurs a little, and I look up at him. "You kept it."

"It's all I had of you." His voice deepens. I reach for the sweater, and without hesitation, he gives it to me. "Jared." My vision blurs again, and his face quivers.

"It's our past, and I won't ever let it go."

I stare at the sweater. No, it's so much more. It scared away the monsters at nighttime. It smells like Jared. Not thinking, I do something I've done a million times. I bring the sweater to my nose and choke on a laugh that escapes me as I inhale the same smell.

Jared.

This is why I grabbed one of Carl's sweaters when they took me in. I had tried to replace Jared's sweater, but nothing and no one would ever replace him. My chest is caving in as I look up at him.

Looking straight ahead, he lets out a breath before getting up again and going to the dresser. His hands seem rigid as he takes something from the top drawer and comes back to me. As he walks a few paces, he doesn't look in my direction. He seems tense and nervous as he hands me a small piece of paper.

He doesn't sit beside me as I glance down at the paper and turn it over. My heart stalls in my chest. I see a girl looking back at me, one I used to know. It's all too much. Slowly, I lift my gaze, and our eyes meet.

"It's the last day I saw you."

My chest squeezes, and I nod as I continue to crumble.

Jared kneels in front of me and extracts the drawing from my hands. He places it on the bed to my left before taking my fingers. My heart triples in speed.

"But now," he says, "this is our future."

A weakness enters my body, and I think this is it; he's going to say he loves me. I don't move or breathe, and a slow grin spreads across Jared's face.

"Breathe, Layla." He says the words softly, and I exhale. His grin widens. "Good girl."

After a moment, Jared's grin disappears. "The day at Mark's beach party... Remember you asked me to make a wish? Did you make a wish?"

I swallow and look down at our joined hands. "Hmm..." I pretend like I have to think about the answer.

Gazing up at him, I feel a bit tongue-tied with the intensity that burns in his brown eyes. The way his head is tilted and how his gaze takes in every inch of my face makes me feel like I'm a treasured painting or someone he's put up on a pedestal for him to gaze at. My pulse spikes, and I sense the fluttering in my neck.

"I wished that your wish would come true," I answer honestly.

His brows rise in surprise, and his dimples appear as he barks out a short laugh. The sound is deep and causes butterflies to erupt in my belly.

"What did you wish for, a million dollars or something like that?" I tease, knowing it wouldn't be money. A hyperawareness of my hand in his hits me as he grows serious.

"A kiss," he says, and I find myself wetting my lips at his words.

"A kiss?" I repeat. Like he hasn't kissed me before? The fact he wished for it makes something about this moment different. "From me?"

"Yes, a kiss," he confirms.

My heart pounds as Jared moves closer. I'm breathing heavily through my nose.

"Are you going to make my wish come true?" The cheeky grin that accompanies his words has me biting my lip. I'd give him so much more than a kiss. I'd give him every single piece of me. Every secret, every wish, every dream, my heart; I'd give him everything. I'd give him all of me.

Jared presses up on his knees, and he lets my fingers go so he can take my face in his large hands. My knees are weak. There's a look in his gaze that I recognize. My hand goes to his shoulder, and before he can kiss me, my truth spills out.

"I love you."

CHAPTER NINE

LAYLA

MY HEART BEATS WILDLY. Blood rushes and roars in my ears as he stares up at me.

He reaches up and touches my cheek. I lean into his touch like it can heal all the broken parts of me, and he stretches a little more. Brown orbs fill my vision before Jared closes his eyes just as our lips touch. His lips are soft and gentle. He applies more pressure, and my hand flutters to his chest. My veins burn, and my body throbs in a way I didn't know was possible. When my lips part slightly under his, electricity flows through me as the tip of his tongue enters my mouth. I inhale sharply at the sensation, giving him more room to deepen the kiss. Our tongues touch, and I tighten my grip on his shirt, pulling him closer.

He's perfect. A part of me thinks I might be dreaming. My brain is screaming for oxygen; it's the only reason I break the kiss. A slight tremor has entered my hands as I cling to Jared. When he opens his eyes and looks at me, a prickly sensation crawls all over me. The fine hairs stand to attention.

"When I was ten, I had this feeling when I looked at you. It was a feeling I didn't understand at the time. I thought it was that I needed to protect you." Jared's fingers trace the outline of my mouth as he speaks. "As I turned twelve, I thought the feeling was because I fancied you. It wasn't until I saw you again that I knew what that feeling was—what it is."

I can't breathe; my heart is going to come out of my chest.

"I love you, Layla. I always have." His forehead touches mine. "Always will," he whispers. I blink, and tears make a pathway down my face. His thumb is there, wiping them away. "Don't cry. Why are you crying?"

I duck my head down, and he follows me, not allowing me to hide. I'm nodding as tears drip off my chin.

I don't want to hide from him. I'm just overwhelmed. I raise my head, and he follows.

"You..." I swallow my emotions as salty liquid finds its way into my mouth. "You were like a superhero to me. During the day, you were there. You always seemed to tower over everything. You cast shadows. You hid me, protected me, and at night, you were there too. Just in a different way. You scared off the monsters. Now in this life, you're fighting for me. Loving me."

I reach up and let my fingers trace his lips, just like he did with me. I'm finding it so hard to tell him what I want to say. "Love just doesn't seem to cover all that I feel. You are everything to me."

Jared has grown still as I speak, and then his mouth finds mine again. The kiss isn't gentle; it's urgent and filled with not just love but loss and tears.

When we break the kiss, Jared rises. With one hand on my chest, he pushes me back onto the bed. The ceiling seems so far away as I stare up at the golden coven. The pattern of small, intricate flowers takes shape the longer I look. My attention is stolen as Jared grabs the material of my dress and slowly slides it up my legs. As he bunches the material, I suck in my stomach and try to drag my legs closer together. Large, warm hands push my legs apart, and I attempt to sit up to see Jared.

"Stay where you are."

I get a glimpse of him before he disappears between my legs. I gasp at the initial contact. His tongue runs along the line of my underpants. Teeth graze my flesh, and I clench my legs around his head. His hands push my thighs back, and he drags down my underpants.

The air is cold against my core as he moves away. I'm aching for him, and when he returns, he doesn't move slowly but plunges his tongue inside me. I want to see him, and I try to look up, but his hand pushes me back down before he reappears. His face is wet. He crawls on top of me, and the air halts in my chest. His tongue flicks out and races across his lips. When he descends over me, he pauses, and I'm aware of how careful he is being with my shoulder.

"I want to try something with you," he says softly.

My heart skips a beat.

He leans down and kisses me. I can taste myself on his lips. His tongue sinks into my mouth, and all I taste is my excitement for him. He breaks the kiss and climbs off me. The bulge in his jeans has a sympathetic agony speeding through me. I want him back. Jared walks to his dresser and opens the second drawer. I can't see what he's doing, but now I wonder if he's getting protection. Am I ready to go the whole way? I love him, yet the thought has my shoulders stiffening. Jared pivots back toward me with a scrap of material in his hand.

His eyes are light and hold a smile at my confusion as he comes back to the bed. He slowly sits me up.

"Trust me," he says before holding up the blindfold that he ties around my head. The room is blackened, and he carefully lies me back on the bed.

My gaze dances behind the blindfold, searching for what will happen next. He's back in between my legs, and before I can react, his tongue runs along my clitoris.

Oh, God.

Jared's fingers run along my legs until they touch my ankles, which he brings up. I feel more exposed. He groans. "So fucking perfect." His words end when he dips his head back down between my legs. I reach down, not sure if I want more or if I want him to stop. But my body arches high, deciding for me.

His tongue leaves my core, and one hand leaves my ankle. The anticipation has me arching a little higher before his fingers dip inside me.

I groan. As his mouth joins his fingers, a current pulses along my flesh. The static races across my chest, pebbling my nipples in his wake, and I feel the pinch along my lips as I bite down while his fingers move faster and harder. Desperation for more has me gripping his head and forcing him deeper. He adds another finger before the rhythm increases, and I release his head. My shoulder burns, and my core throbs painfully. Jared continues to stimulate my pussy, and when he stops, I'm up quickly. Too quickly. I get lightheaded, and I'm reaching for the blindfold, only to be stopped.

"Trust me," he says again.

My heart races, and everything inside me is screaming for release. With his fingers around my wrist, he trails my hand down his chest. The further we go down, the more my excitement builds. I swallow as my fingers graze the large lump in his jeans. He groans, his breath brushing my face, and I want to see him.

I reach for the button of his jeans, feeling brave, but I can't manage it with one hand. Jared's fingers work the button before I hear the zipper. I swallow again, and my heart thumps away in my chest. The material is pushed down, and when I reach out, I touch his large and very erect cock. His groan, this time, sends my head into a spin. I have no idea what I'm doing, but I wrap my fingers around him anyway.

"I want to see you." I release his cock to reach for the blindfold, but he stops me again.

"Leave the blindfold on." He retakes my hand and wraps it around his cock. He moves our hands up and down slowly. His cock bulges, the wetness between my legs continuing to grow with each stroke I give him.

"That's it, baby," Jared croons, and he bends slightly so he can reach me. His hand trails back up under my dress, and I obediently spread my legs with a yearning as he sinks his fingers inside me. His movements are as quick as our hands over his cock. His fingers tighten on mine painfully, but I don't complain as the rhythm grows faster. My body seems locked in a cycle of rapture that I don't want to escape.

My breaths grow faster, and I push myself down on Jared's fingers as we both pump at his cock.

"Oh, fuck!" His groans have my pleasure heightening even further, and I'm moving swiftly over his fingers. His fingers tighten further on mine, cutting off my circulation as he pumps furiously. His groans are cut off, and warm liquid pours over our hands. The sticky substance drips onto my leg, and Jared's fingers loosen over mine as his strokes reduce in speed. The final splash of his cum falls on my leg, and his fingers inside me continue pumping. As he completely takes his hand off mine, I release his cock.

"Lie back." He sounds breathless, but I obey. My body pulsates as Jared runs his tongue along my clit. I'm already so close, and I bring my fingers to my mouth and taste his salty cum. I know I'm close.

I stick my finger into my mouth, wanting to taste Jared again, and it's what breaks my hold. I quiver as I come. I try to pull my legs together as my core vibrates, but Jared is still licking and fucking me with his fingers. He slows with each wave of pleasure that runs through me until they stop. I'm breathless, and my eyes dance frantically behind the blindfold.

"I'll be back in a minute." Jared's words have me nodding. The bed dips as he leaves, and I lie still, trying to allow my heart to find its normal rhythm that it's not quite ready to return to.

A warm washcloth is pressed in between my legs, and when Jared is finished, he runs the cloth along my leg, cleaning up his cum. He takes my hand and cleans it also before he helps me up. My dress is fixed, but I'm aware my panties aren't put back into place.

The bed dips again, and then Jared walks away. I reach up to remove the blindfold, but I can't get it open with one hand.

"Let me." Jared's cologne circles me as he leans in and removes the blindfold.

"You are so beautiful." His words have my heart stalling. I slowly open my eyes. He's so close that if I lean in even slightly, I could kiss him. So I do.

A knock on his door has him stepping away. He grins, and his dimples are on full display as he answers the door.

Words are spoken low, and when Jared turns to me, he's holding two large dessert glasses filled with ice cream.

"Dessert is ready."

I shift to the edge of the bed. "Dessert?" I ask. But I'm wondering when he ordered it.

His cheeky grin accompanies his next words. "I mean, I already had dessert, so this is seconds."

I want to tease too as I slide off the bed. "You are very greedy."

"Greedy?" he questions just before placing a kiss on the tip of my nose. My brain is scrambled from everything that is happening.

We sit down at a small table that mirrors the one in my room. It's nestled between the large open windows. I'm floating and can't stop smiling at Jared. I can still taste salt on my lips, and when I lick them, my cheeks heat. I like the taste of Jared.

"There's a party Friday night. Will you come with me?"

I'm sitting sideways, watching Jared eat his ice cream. I openly ogle him. I don't know why, but he looks different.

He takes the final few scoops out of his dessert, and I assume he's focused on eating and not aware of me. I'm wrong. "Why are you staring at me? I'm not complaining, just curious," he asks.

"It's just nice to watch you without worrying about you noticing," I answer honestly, even as heat rises in my cheeks.

"You used to watch me?" he sounds amused. He glances at me, his grin so self-assured.

I roll my eyes. "Sometimes. But don't let it go to your head," I tease.

"Too late. It's gone to my head."

I laugh.

"So, will you come with me?"

My first reaction is that I need to ask Carl and Evelyn, but that's not necessary. "Yeah, of course."

"As my girlfriend."

My heart leaps at his words and deep voice. He looks at me with uncertainty, as if I might say no. I know that no isn't an option. But right now, I don't want it to be an option.

"Yes. Yes, of course."

"Great." The smile that accompanies his words tells me he's very happy about my acceptance.

I have a boyfriend. And not just any boyfriend, but Jared.

***

It's been two days since I told Jared I love him and he said it back. Since then, we've spent every second together. But behind all the smiles and laughs, along with our roaming hands, I can't stop thinking about Evelyn and Carl. So today, I'm going home to visit. Jared isn't exactly happy about it, but I didn't think he would be.

When I arrive home, the moment is tense. I'm alone, as I asked Jared to give me some space.

I took another huge bite of stir-fry after announcing I was dating Jared and going to a party with him. It lodges itself in my throat, and it takes half a glass of water just to wash it down.

Evelyn sets her knife and fork on the plate while joining her hands together, her elbows resting on the table.

"You're dating Jared?" she questions with her head tilted.

I quickly glance at Carl, who isn't eating either. I nod. "Yeah, I am."

Carl clears his throat. "Since when?" No one sounds happy.

"A few days." They glance at each other, and straight away, I think I should have kept that small bit of information to myself.

"A few days?" Evelyn's ordinarily level voice is high pitched. I swallow. "Yeah."

Evelyn picks up her knife and fork and starts back into her dinner. Carl and I watch her. I think that this can't be it, no more questions. She's cutting into her meat like it's livestock, not a soft piece of chicken. Carl covers her hand with his, stopping her, and they have a conversation with their eyes, which is something I've seen them do before. A part of me wants to leave, but I wait until Evelyn looks up at me.

"This party. Where is it?"

"It's at one of Jared's friends' houses."

Evelyn doesn't look sure, and my stomach plummets. I want her to be happy for me so badly. "Morgan is coming with me," I blurt out.

"Morgan's nice," Carl says while nodding, as if he's trying to convince himself of that fact.

Silence from Evelyn. I squirm in my seat as she watches me.

"This is your first boyfriend." Her tone has softened, but my face burns at her statement. She isn't going to do this in front of Carl. I want to crawl under the table, and by the looks of it, so does Carl.

"As long as your mother is happy, you have my blessing. You're a good kid." Carl's words run deep into me, seeping into my soul. I don't think he understands the impact his words have. Evelyn's eyes glisten, and I can see she knows what his words mean to me.

"You're growing up too fast," Evelyn finally says. Her words are low, but she's smiling. This is a moment I didn't think would ever happen to me. Where parents would use a line like, *You're growing up too fast*. I dreamt about it, fantasized about it, and now it's real.

"So, is Morgan picking you up?" Carl has started to eat again, which is a good sign.

"Actually, I'm picking her up," I say, and I pray that when I text her and tell her that she isn't just going to a party but going with me, that she'll agree to it. Carl and Evelyn exchange more looks.

"Okay," Evelyn says.

We eat in silence. Evelyn keeps stealing glances at me, and I know she has so many questions. I hate that she appears older. Have I done that to her?

"He's really good to me," I confess, and both Evelyn and Carl stop eating. "He treats me like a queen," I admit as my eyes burn.

"I've never wanted anything so badly." I'm trying to make them understand. "I love both of you so much."

"That's what scares me, Layla." Evelyn gets up, and my heart deflates as I think she's going to leave, but she stops at my chair and pulls me into a hug. She's still so careful with my shoulder.

"I'm trying so hard," she whispers into my ear. For now, that will have to be enough.

When Evelyn releases me, she sends Carl and me into the sitting room as she gets dessert. I tell Carl about Jared's father and how nice he is. The conversation flows as Evelyn returns with pavlova and strawberries. My favorite.

I take out my phone as we all eat and watch TV. I need to text Morgan and keep Evelyn and Carl happy. It's a small question, but my nerves fly through me as I text her.

Party Friday night. Will you come with me?

I don't have to wait long for Morgan to respond.

Yeah, cool. What time?

Relief swims through my veins, and I sag briefly. My fingers move over the keys.

Can I borrow a dress?

I have nothing to wear. My wardrobe at Jared's is filled with gowns, and I need something more casual, but I also want to make an effort. And since I'm going as Jared's girlfriend, I want to look good. My phone buzzes in my hand. Morgan's name flashes up on the screen. I answer the call.

"What have you done with Layla?" she asks, suspicion in her voice.

"I just want to look nice," I tell her. Evelyn and Carl glance my way. "It's Morgan," I say, covering the microphone.

"It will take some work. But..." The insult isn't lost on me, but I'm on a high and nothing is going to take me down.

"Morgan," I warn and am surprised at the small chuckle that resonates through the phone line.

"We can get dressed together." Her words sound nervous. Getting ready with Morgan isn't exactly something I want to do. "Or not," she says, her voice snappy.

"No. We can do that. Friday night around eight?"

"Great, I'll see you then."

Great.

I hang up. "Is it okay if I get ready here Friday night?" I ask. Evelyn wrestles with a smile. "Of course."

CHAPTER TEN

JARED

IT'S OUR FIRST DAY back on campus, and everything about this moment feels right. Layla, in a pair of black skinny jeans, is slowly killing me.

"If you aren't ready, we can stay at home." I reach for her leg and give it a squeeze.

She grins. "We need to get back to school." She has more use of her arm, but her movements are slow as she unclips her belt. I lean in and steal a kiss. Her gaze darts to me. Her smile widens and my cock grows hard.

"I'm not sure I can get used to this," Layla says, ducking her head.

"Used to what?" I try to catch her gaze.

"Us."

I tip her chin up. "It's always been 'us.' It's never been any other way, even when we were apart."

Layla's attention leaves me. I follow her stare to see my friends watching my car. *Friends.* I use that word so fucking loosely. I'm already about to pound anyone who even looks funny at Layla. I see Warren, and I want to have a word with him.

"Are you sure about this?" I ask Layla again.

"Yes." She reaches for the door handle while gripping her bag in her other hand, and I watch her slide off the passenger seat, enjoying the view of her perfect ass.

I rearrange my erection before getting out of the vehicle. My friends move closer. Mark is the first to reach me, and he smiles while giving me a fist bump.

"Great to have our leader back." He grins.

Alex, Abby, and Caroline make their way to Layla, and they gush compliments over her outfit. Layla's eyebrows rise, and she searches for me. When our gazes clash, I walk to her and entwine our fingers together. The girls stop cackling, but Alex, always the professional, carries on the discussion a few seconds later, chattering like this isn't odd. Warren flicks a half-smoked cigarette on the ground and leans against his own car. The red BMW has been upgraded with all the specs. I want to talk to him but remember that I'm here with Layla. I jut out my chin in greeting, and he pushes off his car. He walks over and fist-bumps me.

"Thought you'd fucked off." He grins while taking a pack of cigarettes out of his pocket and lighting one up.

"Well..." he greets Layla.

"Hi." Her voice is small.

"This is Warren," I say.

Warren grins before blowing smoke into the air.

"I'm Layla." Layla takes her hand out of mine and holds it out to Warren, who takes it with a grin on his face.

"You new here?" he asks while releasing her hand.

Alex and her sidekicks talk fashion, but I can sense Alex's attention on us. Mark steps up beside Warren.

"Yeah, I transferred halfway through the year," Layla tells him.

"You like it?" Warren asks while blowing smoke in Mark's direction.

Mark coughs, and I swear Warren grins.

Layla glances up at me before she answers. "Yeah. It's a nice school."

I spot Ashley and Lucas in the distance. I harden my stare, and they scurry the fuck off. I don't want them near Layla. I retake her hand.

"Rex was wondering about you," Warren says.

"Are you still training with him?" I'm surprised Warren has stuck it out for so long.

"Yeah, he busts my balls. But it keeps my uncle happy."

I want to ask which uncle in particular. His uncles are notorious in this area. I've never met them in person, but if the opportunity arose, I'd snap it up.

Mark points at Warren. "Didn't one of your uncles own this place?" Mark asks, and Alex and her friends stop talking. What the fuck is wrong with Mark?

Warren drops his cigarette and crushes it under his boot. He glares up at Mark, and I don't want any shit to go down.

"They still do." Warren grins.

That's news to me. I don't comment, but it's something I'll ask my dad about. Maybe he's in partnership with them. It doesn't seem likely, but honestly, I don't care.

"I better get to class," Layla says softly.

I squeeze Layla's fingers, and the group breaks up as I walk with her to class.

I spot Ashley to my right and tighten my hold on Layla.

"You don't have to walk me to class," she says.

I grin. "I want to walk my girlfriend to class."

She can't hide her smile, even as she ducks her head into her chest. I don't think she notices Ashley as we pass her. I give her a look that tells her to stay the fuck away. I don't want her anywhere near Layla. I part with Layla at her classroom door. She fidgets with her hands as everyone watches us, and I know she doesn't like the attention. I've never thought anything of always being watched, until now. I want time with Layla. Being at home was perfect. Here, reality has come crashing back.

"I'll be here when class is over," I promise as she enters her business class.

I return outside in search of Warren, but he's not there. Taking out my phone, I ring him and the sound of a cell phone comes from around the corner. I walk along the wall, the ringing growing louder, and when I'm nearly to the sound, I hang up. I find Warren, but he's not alone. A girl is on her knees giving him a blow job.

He notices me and holds up his index finger. The brunette doesn't stop, and I walk back around the side of the building. A few people pass me, and I grin when I hear their surprise. I bet Warren hasn't even stopped. It takes another five minutes before he appears. The brunette runs off into the building, looking very happy with herself while she wipes her mouth with the back of her hand.

"I needed that," Warren says as he lights up a cigarette.

"Do you have any news for me?" I ask, leaning against the wall.

Warren pockets his lighter and runs his hand through his hair. "Yeah, I got that sorted for you."

I push off the wall. "Are you serious?" I ask. I want him to be serious. He looks serious.

"He wants fifty grand."

I nod. Money is no problem. Warren reaches into his pocket and passes me a scrap of paper. "That's the account number." I take it and open the paper.

Warren's watching me. "You know there's no going back after doing this." His eyes are haunted, and I wonder about Warren's life with the O'Reagans. Has he ever taken a life? And if so, did he get his hands dirty or pay someone else to pull the trigger?

"Good," I answer. "The money will be wired today."

"Did you find your man?" Warren asks.

"Not yet. But I will." My PI still hasn't found Chester. The fucker is hiding, but he'll have to come out, eventually. I promised Layla I wouldn't shoot Chester, but that doesn't stop me from hiring someone else to kill him for me.

"I'd better get to class." I fist-bump Warren before walking away. I have no intentions of going to class. Instead, I take a detour to the dean's office. His door is open, and I knock once before entering.

"Welcome back, Mr. McGivney." He doesn't seem overly pleased to see me, but I don't give two fucks.

I close the door behind me and walk deeper into the office. I don't take a seat but stuff my hands into my pockets. "Lucas and Sam Garcia need to be removed from the school."

The dean exhales and leans back in his chair, pressing the end of his pen to his chin. "And why would that happen?"

I want to say because I fucking said so. "Because Sam is dealing drugs out of his car," I lie.

He was hanging with Chester the night Layla was at Chester's home, and so was Sam.

"That's a matter for the Gardaí." The dean sits forward, placing his pen on the table.

"If you bring the Gardaí here, I'm sure they'll find a few cars with gear in them." He knows this, so I'm not sure why he's stalling.

"And the reason that Lucas should be removed?" He waits.

"He's been harassing some of the female students." I picture him stalking Layla. The dean doesn't answer, and I remove my hands from my pockets. "I want their scholarships revoked," I say clearly. I'd pull Ashley's too, but I don't want to upset Layla.

"If I were to leave here"—the dean steeples his fingers into the desk—"and check Sam Garcia's car, I would find drugs?"

I sneer. "No. But if that's what you want, I can make it happen."

He finally understands what I'm saying.

"I want it done today." I leave on that note and burn through the rest of the time allotted for class by ringing my PI. Still no news on Chester. I check in with all my security. Once again, there has been nothing unusual. That doesn't sit well with me.

Lunchtime comes around, and I wait outside Layla's class. She smiles when she sees me, and I eagerly take her hand as Ashley waves at her.

"See you later, Ashley," Layla says.

"You know she used to date Chester," I tell her.

Layla's body grows rigid, and I hate doing this to her, but she needs to keep away from Ashley. I have no idea what the girl is capable of or what she might do for Chester. She could lure Layla away from the safety of the school.

"Yes, I know she dated Chester. That doesn't make her a bad person," Layla defends straight away. "Stupid, yes. But not bad."

I pull her closer to the wall, and we stop walking. "Just hear me out. He might use her to get to you."

She's shaking her head. "She wouldn't do that."

I lean in closer. "How well do you know her? *Really* know her, Layla?"

Doubt clouds Layla's gaze, and she chews on her lip. I quickly press a kiss to her mouth. "I don't want you to worry, but I also want you to be aware. Okay?"

She nods.

I feel far more assured as I take Layla into the full cafeteria so everyone can see we're together. I don't want any other guy so much as looking at her with interest. This makes it clear. She's mine.

CHAPTER ELEVEN

LAYLA

WILD THOUGHTS SPIN IN my mind as I enter the cafeteria with Jared. He has no idea how magnetic he is. He's a force that draws everyone's attention. Their gazes hover over me with curiosity, but it's Jared that holds their interest. I glance up at him. He's nodding greetings at people, and he walks with such confidence. I could never possess that type of surety. Even as a kid, he was charismatic. It's not something anyone is taught; they're just born with it.

His fingers tighten on mine, and I take comfort in his touch. Alex and her two friends move ahead of us and grab the one table in the center of the cafeteria that's remained empty. Every other table is taken, and as we join them, I wonder if it's held for them.

Alex smiles, and I'm waiting for her to turn on me. It's such a negative thought, and I try to brush it away. Mark sits across from us, and two other guys join in.

"This is Simon and Gary," Jared says while releasing my hand. I fold both on my lap.

"What's up?" Simon asks. His long hair is swept back over one shoulder. He's built like a quarterback. Gary jerks his chin out at me.

"Hi." I feel so self-conscious, like the girl who shouldn't be sitting with the cool kids.

"I'll be right back." Jared gets up, but before he leaves, he presses a kiss to the top of my head.

I freeze under the affection and how everyone watches. Once he's gone, I'm waiting for the wolves to circle.

"So, the girls and I are going to go shopping after school to get a dress for the party. Do you want to come?" Alex asks.

I'm stumped at being invited. "I have loads of dresses," I say.

"Yeah, but it's an excuse to get a new one," Caroline says sweetly.

Alex smiles. "What she said."

I'm not buying that Alex likes me for one second. Jared reappears carrying a tray of food. I glance over at the very long line that he's privileged enough to skip. He sits down. A sandwich and tea are placed in front of me. He reaches into his pocket and extracts a red apple that he hands to me before taking a bread roll and his own tea off the tray.

"Thanks."

"So, what do you think?" Alex asks.

I blink a few times, feeling overwhelmed with all this.

"About what?" Jared asks, and he sounds defensive.

"The girls and I are going dress shopping for the party, and we invited Layla to join us."

I take a quick peek at Jared, wondering if he wants me to go. These are his friends, and they're making an effort.

"I'd love to," I answer.

Caroline claps, and Abby forces a smile. She's the only one who isn't pretending this is normal, and I like her for that.

"Great. We can go in my car after school," Alex says.

I nod before I back out and open the packaging from around my sandwich. It's hard to eat knowing everyone is watching us, and by the time we leave the cafeteria, I'm exhausted. Jared takes my hand again, and we walk ahead of the rest of his friends.

"How do you do this all the time?" I ask out of the corner of my mouth as Jared continues to nod and greet all the passing students. "How can you know everyone?" I add.

"I don't know everyone. They just know who I am."

I glance up at Jared. "Don't you ever get tired?" I couldn't do this daily. I mean, this was one day in the life of Jared, and I'm ready for bed.

"I don't ever think about it."

We stop at my classroom door. "How do you know what class I have?" I'm suspicious, but Jared seems to know everything.

"I may have broken into the dean's office and copied your schedule."

"Jared." *Jesus, if he got caught...*

He laughs. "I checked your schedule this morning before we left."

"Oh." Of course he did. It was in my backpack.

"I won't see you after class since you're going shopping with Alex and the girls?" It's more of a question than a statement. Jared pulls me in close to the wall to let several students pass. They gawk, and I try not to let their stares bother me.

"She's making an effort. So I should too."

Jared tilts up my chin. "You don't have to, Layla."

"I want to." I do. I want to try for him.

He plants a soft kiss on my lips. Even though it's soft, I feel it all the way down to my toes.

"I'll see you later, then."

The room's full, and I take the only vacant seat. Even though Jared is no longer with me, everyone still stares. All of a sudden, I'm visible to these people. Only a few days ago, I was a nobody.

Class ends, and with it comes the end of the day. Alex, Abby, and Caroline are waiting for me outside the building. Jared is there too, and I hate how my body sighs at the sight of him. He said he wouldn't be here. My body leans toward him, like he can take away the uncertainty I'm harboring about going shopping.

Caroline wears a look of pure joy. "This is going to be such fun."

Jared steps closer to me, and I take his outstretched hand as he pulls me into his body. "I can take you if you want," he offers with a slight raise of a brow.

I bite my lip. How I would love that. "No. Like Caroline said, it will be fun."

Jared fights a grin, but a dimple makes an appearance. I'm tempted to touch the indent.

"We aren't going to eat her." Alex tries to sound playful, but irritation circles her words.

Jared presses a kiss to my lips. It's light and featherlike, but it doesn't stop the kiss from sneaking past my defenses.

I inhale all of him as he releases me.

Jared addresses the three ladies who he holds in rapt attention. "She better come back to me in one piece."

"Don't worry, she will." Caroline smiles sweetly.

It's too sweet.

I release Jared's hand.

Alex rolls her eyes. "We'll have her back in better condition than we got her in." Alex exhales before her lips curl back, displaying snow-white teeth.

Stepping away from Jared and the trio isn't a smooth transition, but I'm proud when I don't look back as we walk to Alex's car.

Alex drives, and I get to ride shotgun.

"So, Layla, do you have any color in mind?" Caroline pipes up from the back seat. I open my mouth to answer but don't get to as she continues to ask questions, not leaving room for me to actually answer her. "I think red would suit you. Or maybe blue. Like your eyes." My seat is jerked back as she grips the headrest to pull herself forward. Her face is near mine. "You have such pretty eyes."

I take a peek at Alex. She appears relaxed, but it's the permanent smile on her face that's concerning. She reminds me of a Stepford wife.

"Thank you," I answer Caroline and try not to fidget.

"Anytime." Caroline sits back. The click of her belt is deafening in the quiet car.

We drive in silence to the mall. I'm regretting my decision to come with them, but I remind myself that I am doing this for Jared. These are his friends, and I need to make an effort.

"I appreciate you asking me to come along," I tell the girls.

"Absolutely," Alex says.

"What are friends for?" Caroline grips my seat again, and I can see that becoming annoying pretty quickly. Abby is the only one who isn't over the top.

The mall is thronged, and I'm already uncomfortable. We have to swivel around shoppers, and staying together isn't easy, which delights me. That is, until Caroline finds me and takes my hand in hers.

"We don't want you disappearing." The lazy smile lifts her pink-painted lips.

"I won't." My words are lost as she pulls me through the crowd while she sings pretty apologies to make people move out of her way.

We take a quick right and step into a shop that has barely no shoppers and lots of space. I can already tell this is going to be expensive. I have my purse with me, but my budget won't stretch as far as the price tags.

Caroline still holds my hand, and I wiggle my fingers out of her grasp. I don't make eye contact but walk away and hope I can get lost in the spaced-out racks. What a waste of floor space.

"Since it's just you and me, I think we need to cut the crap." Alex speaks while shifting a dress shirt aside. She takes out a pinstripe skirt and holds it up before putting it back on the rack. "I'm doing this for Jared. Not you." She continues to move clothes around, wearing her Stepford-wife smile.

I move to the rack beside her and do the exact thing, mimicking her motions. "Funny, I'm doing this for Jared as well."

Our gazes clash, and all I see is hate burning away in hers.

I don't hate Alex. I'm weary of her.

She reaches into the rack, and without looking, pulls out a green dress. "You should try this on."

She keeps it held out, and when I take it, she walks off.

God, I was a fool to come here with them.

A squeal erupts as I spin to come face-to-face with Caroline.

"Oh my God, I didn't mean to scare you. She's being super mean." Caroline twirls a lock of brown hair around her finger. She leans in. "I like you."

I have no idea if she means that or if this is all part of her and Alex's grand plan.

"Thanks." I sound unsure.

Caroline doesn't seem to notice. She releases her lock of hair and spins on the tip of her toes. "Let's find you a dress and blow Jared's socks off."

Her humor steals a smile from me.

I end up in the fitting room with six dresses. Caroline picked three of them, I picked one, and two are from Alex. The girls hover in the fitting room as I strip out of my clothes. I start with Caroline's dress, a blue one. She was right, it compliments my eyes. Confidence has me pulling back the curtain. Alex and Caroline straighten up. Abby remains in a slumped position like she'd rather be watching paint dry.

"Wow! Jared's socks will be officially blown," Caroline declares.

She's so unaffected by the narrowed gaze Abby makes in her direction or how Alex's smile widens, making her face appear ready to crack.

I lose some of my enthusiasm and try on four more dresses, including the one I selected.

They don't get much of a reaction from Caroline as she declares that the first blue dress is the one.

I'm avoiding trying on the one that Alex chose. It's to the floor, frumpy, and just has no shape. The color—I'm tempted to say it's mud brown—is ugly. But I still put it on and step out of the fitting room.

Caroline's gaze widens in horror, but Alex rises from her seat and clicks her fingers. Abby sits up, and I'm concerned with her sudden rise from her slumber.

"I love it," Abby deadpans.

I pretend I buy her lie.

"What she said. It's perfect." Alex claps her hands happily, and if I didn't know her, I'd think she was genuinely happy for me.

"I'm not sure." I turn and pretend to take a second look in the mirror. I could take a hundred looks, and the dress would still be ugly.

"I mean, it's cute." Caroline's words are pained before they lower. "I did love the blue one."

"Don't be so cruel, Caroline. She can't wear the blue one," Alex snaps.

"Why not?" Caroline sounds confused, and so am I.

I face the trio. Is this a case where she's wearing blue so nobody else can wear blue?

"You know why. Layla doesn't want to show off her grotesque leg." Alex flings a glance at me real quick. "No offense." She turns back to Caroline, a smirk crawling on her lips. "I doubt that would blow his socks off. More like having him keep them on."

Pain starts in the center of my chest and spreads at an alarming pace. Heat races up my throat, and I hate the look Abby wears.

Pity.

She's pitying the girl with the deformed leg. I want to crawl back into the fitting room but find myself robotically moving while Alex declares we've found the winning dress.

CHAPTER TWELVE

LAYLA

LAST NIGHT AFTER COMING back from shopping with the girls, I went straight to my room with a headache. Amanda, Andrea, and Kerry parked themselves outside my room, and once I mentioned a headache, I was shuffled into bed with two painkillers and a damp cloth across my eyes.

I appreciated their attention, as it kept Jared away for a while. He wasn't happy and had entered even as Kerry insisted I needed my rest.

"Is everything okay?" he asked.

I pressed the cloth against my eyes. "A headache. I suffer with them sometimes." It was easier to lie with the cotton cloth covering most of my face.

"Are you sure? What about dress shopping?" He shifted beside my bed.

"I got a dress."

He was silent, and I just wanted him to leave.

"Okay, I'll let you rest," he said after a moment.

I didn't move the cloth until the bedroom door closed, and I stayed hidden in my room like a coward for the night.

***

The scent of peanut butter in Jared's car has me raising a brow at him. His laugh pulls a silly grin onto my face, and yesterday's ordeal seems unworthy of the attention I gave it last night.

"I made sandwiches," he confesses before starting the car and pulling out of the garage. I'm shaking my head while grinning, but my heart is all over the place.

"You made peanut butter sandwiches," I say, and when Jared glances at me this time, he isn't smiling, and my chest squeezes. Is he remembering back to Lucas giving me one? Funny how that led to my first kiss with Jared and him nearly drowning me.

"I made them just in case you were hungry." He focuses on the road. He says it so offhandedly, as if we aren't going to pass several restaurants or stores. He made them because it's something else we share.

He still amazes me. I glance out the window before looking back at him. An overwhelming feeling to reach out and touch his hand has me stuffing mine between my legs. My knees bobble, and I look out the window. I hate how many emotions swirl uncontrollably inside me.

I focus on all the houses we pass, trying to force my body to relax. I close my eyes and try not to think of each time we shared a peanut butter sandwich. I glance over at him, realizing I've been holding my breath while fighting tears.

"You don't have to eat it if you don't want to." He says this after a moment, and I wonder if his mind has gone where mine has.

I'm making this seem like I'm ungrateful, when really, the stupid sandwich is making my heart hammer. "No. I want it," I say.

His dimples appear before he speaks. "I knew you couldn't resist a peanut butter sandwich. If I ever wanted to kidnap you, all I would have to do is leave a trail of them from your door all the way to my car," he teases.

"You wouldn't need to do that. I'd come without the sand-wiches."

Our gazes connect, and I see a look on Jared's face that I recognize. Happiness.

Jared pulls over after only an hour of driving. We're in a parking lot overlooking the beach. It's a strip of the beach I've been to before. He reaches into the back seat, the scent of his aftershave feeding my hungry lungs. He's so close that I have to look out the window before I do something crazy, like sniff him. How many times has he openly inhaled me? Did he ever have the same tornado of emotions spinning out of control like I do?

Once he sits back, he opens the bag and takes out the sandwich and a bottle of water. Handing me one, he smiles. I unwrap the foil, thinking about how he took the time to make this sandwich, wrap it for me, and put it in the bag. A lump forms in my throat.

"Thank you."

"What's wrong?" His own sandwich sits in his hand, the bottle of water between his legs.

"Nothing's wrong, it's just so nice."

Relief sweeps over Jared's face. As an afterthought, he smirks and takes a bite of his sandwich. "I'm a nice guy," he says. The cockiness in his voice has me snorting a laugh.

I open my sandwich, telling myself to stop being sentimen-tal. Taking a bite, I sink back into my seat, exaggerating how tasty it is. I ignore the thump of my heart as Jared laughs.

"That's it. I'm keeping a stash of them in my car. Every time you get in, you're eating one."

"I won't argue." I take another bite before looking out at the beach. Not many are around, but you can already tell that today will be unseasonably hot. It's hard to believe that only a few weeks ago we were at another beach.

For the first time, I think of Kieran. Taking a drink, I wash down the sandwich and the guilt I still feel about that day. The image of Jared's violence flashes in my mind, and I take a peek at him. He seems content as he eats his sandwich. There's an uncomfortable feeling in the pit of my stomach when I think of his rage, how far gone he looked that day.

I resume trying to eat but glance at him sideways. He's looking out at the beach, chewing the last of his sandwich. His hands rest on his lap; he appears relaxed. His black T-shirt clings to him, and my gaze trails down to the necklace that disappears under the T-shirt. I know a key hangs on the end, another mystery about Jared I don't understand.

"So, how are you?" I ask and am surprised by how much his body tenses. His jaw grows tight. Is he thinking about the night at the beach too?

He crumbles up the foil, his focus on the shiny material like it holds all the answers. "I'm good. Why do you ask?"

He sounds so defensive. *Is he mad at me?*

"I'm sorry." I look up at Jared, and he's watching me, brows furrowed like he's confused. "About everything," I add. "I just..."

The waves break against the shoreline, and I focus on them. "So much has happened since I came here and"—I shrug—"I feel responsible." He crinkles the foil again, and without thought, I take it from his hand.

"I mean, I didn't force Chester to shoot me, but yeah, other stuff." This is coming out all wrong.

"Like what?" Jared reaches out and takes his foil back. He keeps clenching the ball in his fist.

"I'm thinking of Kieran," I spit out.

His lips drag down as he jerks his head. "Kieran?"

God, he sounds pissed. His gaze darkens, and he's waiting for me to explain myself.

"You were so angry," I whisper.

"You kissed him, Layla. I was homicidal."

"That's what every girl wants to hear," I say without thinking.

His grin makes no sense. "I was jealous. So we took a few swings at each other. Boys fight. You have nothing to feel guilty about. Kieran and I are cool now. In fact, he apologized." Hearing his words helps the guilt I felt sprout wings and fly away.

"So yeah," he murmurs before glancing away. "All's good."

I take the foil out of his hand, and his brows rise. I have no idea why I keep taking it back. Maybe so I can be closer to him. This time, when Jared takes the foil out of my hand, our fingers brush slightly. The contact causes my pulse to skip. I shift back at the unexpected feeling that takes over all my senses. Jared doesn't seem to notice my reaction as he stuffs the foil into the brown paper bag.

As he puts on his seat belt, I focus on putting on mine and dispel the want to have him right here and now. "Well, if you ever want to talk, you know I'm here." This time, he observes me slowly. The shift of his gaze over my face has me forcing myself to stay still.

"I know you are. Thanks." His long, tanned fingers entwine with mine, and I focus on our hands. This isn't the first time he's done this, so I don't know why it feels more intimate. Maybe it's my thoughts, the two of us alone in his car over-looking the beach. Or maybe it's how his eyes seem more golden than I've ever seen them before. The dimples are out now in full force, and my lips twitch before turning into a smile.

"I'm here for you, too," Jared says, still looking at me and smiling.

"I know." A man passes in front of the car and catches my attention briefly. It isn't the man, but the huge St. Bernard he has with him. As I watch them pass, I don't say anything, just smile. When I was little, I always said that when I grew up, I would have one.

"Still want one?" Jared asks the question, along with a slight squeeze of our still joined hands.

Glancing from the dog and back to Jared, I'm not complete-ly surprised that he remembered.

"Yeah, I still want one. I just have more sense now to know it might not be viable." I stare at our joined hands. The contrast of my pale skin to his tanned fascinates me.

"You do know they slobber everywhere, right?"

My gaze flickers up to Jared's, and I smile. "Yes, I do. Do you know that—"

"They can die of a broken heart," Jared finishes my sen-tence. The amusement in his eyes has my cheeks turning pink.

"Well, did you know the St. Bernard got its name from a snowy pass in the Alps? That type of dog was used to rescue stranded travelers in snowstorms in the Great St. Bernard Pass between Italy and Switzerland and earned its name that way." More amusement flashes across Jared's face, this time with a raised eyebrow.

"You're full of facts, Layla Jordan."

The world around me grows fuzzy. It's been such a long time since I heard my old surname. Although I'm elated Jared remembers, it also reminds me of my life with Bert and Ron-nie. Avoiding Jared's gaze, I remove my hand from his. My palms grow damp with sweat, and I don't want him to notice.

After a couple of silent moments, Jared asks quietly, "Have I upset you?"

"No, it just surprised me a little. I haven't heard that name in so long." I speak while staring out the window. The sky has grown overcast, promising a downpour of rain. That's Ireland for you. One minute the sun is splitting the stones, and the next it's a washout.

"Layla, I'm sorry. I didn't think."

When I feel more in control, I glance at Jared. His expres-sion is unreadable as he leans against the steering wheel. His head rests on his arms, and his eyes have darkened.

"Don't be. I need to learn to control my reaction," I say. As I speak, my brows drag together. Can I ever control my reaction to a past that terrifies me? The sound of a seat belt unbuckling has me turning to Jared. He's so close, our noses nearly touch. My heart pounds like I've run up and down the beach that sprawls out in front of us.

"I..." I'm not sure what I even want to say. He's there. His gaze roams my face, and he wears such a serious look. I swallow.

"If you feel sad, be sad. If you feel happy, be happy. If you want to scream, then do it." Jared's voice grows with each word, and I smile at how passionate he sounds. But he doesn't mirror my smile. Instead, his warm hands grip my face until I think my heart will explode right there and then.

"Stop apologizing for how you feel. This"—his eyes travel across my face—"is perfect and I love how real and honest you always are. So don't try to hide anything."

The heat of his hands on my face has to be the cause of the sudden increase in temperature. The air feels hot as Jared continues to invade my space. I'm breathing heavily through my nose, and all I can do is nod as I inhale the scent that is uniquely his, along with his cologne and warm breath. Jared bites down on his lower lip, the movement capturing my attention.

The sensation starts to build, as it had earlier. A voice in the back of my head tells me this isn't good at all. I need distance, but I can't seem to move. I do, however, break eye contact, and that has Jared releasing me. He sits back in his seat, and I try to settle my heart down. Rain pelts against the windshield. The beach has disappeared now. Only colors are visible with the onslaught of rain.

I swallow, realizing I need to say something. I can't let this get awkward.

"That gray wool sweater that you loved... I used to steal it at night." The confession is abrupt, and I want to sink into the seat.

What is wrong with me?

"When you came to my room each night, I would pretend to be asleep so you could take it," Jared says.

I look at him. He isn't looking at me but out the window. Sadness shadows him, and my throat burns. He knew and had let me take it. It was his favorite sweater.

"I used to smell it at night, so it was like you were there with me." My eyes burn.

"I would have stayed with you, Layla. Why didn't you just ask?" His raised voice carries a harsh tone and causes my wet eyes to dry up.

"I was a child, Jared. Why are you so angry?"

"Because... I just... I would have stayed with you." His own eyes glaze as he grits his teeth.

"You were like my big brother. I didn't think you would."

Jared looks away, his grip tightening on the steering wheel until his knuckles turn white. "What were you afraid of?" His question is asked of the beach, then his gaze flickers across to me. I can see his pulse pound in his neck.

"I was afraid..." I say, trying to think back to what scared me so much. The dark? The teddies were old and too high on the shelf for me to remove. I always thought they were looking at me.

"Of what?" Once again, Jared's whispering, his whole body tight with tension.

"The dark, Jared. Wasn't there anything you were afraid of?" I ask, and it's like a hand reaches in and pushes him against the seat. The movement startles me.

"No, what could I have been afraid of? The dark? I'm not a girl." The quick words and forced smile have me sitting up even straighter.

His body relaxes now as he cracks his knuckles. It's the first time I've seen him do it since I've met him again. He's forcing himself to relax. I've seen him do it before, but as a child, I didn't understand it.

"Jared."

At his name, he finally looks at me. "I just wish you had told me. I would have scared away the dark." He smiles, and I push away my uncertainty.

"Your sweater did the trick. We didn't need you."

His laugh at my words and the dimples that appear relax me further.

"We?" he questions.

"Yeah, me and your sweater. It was more like a teddy. So I named him."

"You named my sweater?"

My face heats up, but I don't care. I'm just so happy that he's happy again. That darkness has left his eyes. Now they shine, the gold flecks lightening up.

"Mr. Grey."

His laughter has me joining him. I don't know if it's been the heaviness of before, but we end up laughing loudly. When we settle down, I feel better. Lighter.

"I'm glad Mr. Grey kept you safe at night," he says.

"Yeah, he did." I think how safe I felt with Jared's smell and the warmth of Mr. Grey. I was untouchable. It was my safe place.

"I hope you and Mr. Grey didn't get up to anything else."

I narrow my eyes at Jared. His grin stretches across his handsome face.

"I was ten!" I exclaim.

Jared chuckles again while buckling up his belt. "We better get moving." When the wipers come on, the view of the beach is beautiful. The rain still falls. The sky is purple and blue against the water. I keep watching the waves crash as Jared starts the car, and we make our way to the garden show.

CHAPTER THIRTEEN

LAYLA

Hundreds of people mill about the indoor garden center. I take one final look down at my dress. It's a bit crumpled from the car ride, but with the heat in the building, the creases are sure to fall out. Jared's fingers twine with mine.

"You look perfect. Come on." A small tug and an encouraging smile from him have me moving.

The hanging baskets that conceal the ceiling above us give the first section a magical and even secretive feel. The exhibition is broken up into different segments. Right now we're in the flower section. Ceramic flower pots and seller stands create a zig-zag path that is overcrowded. I can hear water in the distance. The heat from all the people so close has me moving faster toward the sound, but at a snail's pace. We end up being stopped at the cactus section. The baby ones that are no bigger than my thumb are so cute.

"They're adorable," I say.

Jared snorts, causing the woman in the oversized white hat to look back at him. Her jacket and tailored pants must have been sweltering. I'm glad about my choice of dress.

Jared stands up on the tip of his toes to see what the holdup is.

"Anything?" I ask. He shakes his head. "I can't see what's causing the jam. Only more people and plants."

I grin. "How odd. People and plants at a garden exhibition." Jared narrows his eyes but smirks.

"Yeah, as odd as that thing." We're already standing pretty close to each other, so when he reaches behind me, his chest brushes against my shoulder. The contact has my pulse spiking. It takes me a moment after he leans back to focus on what he holds. The baby cactus.

"It's not odd. I think it's cute," I say.

"We'll see how cute it is when you touch it," he says.

The woman once again turns, looking at the cactus, then from me to Jared.

"Do you want to touch it?" he asks, and she swings back around. His hand curves slightly around the cactus. I don't think he knows what he's doing. He's protecting it.

"Ouch."

I grin as he quickly opens his hand.

"You find that funny?"

"It's so tiny, and you're so..."

His grin rises quick and fast. "So..." he encourages, and my mind goes back to his room, and with it the memory of my hand wrapped around his cock. My heart pitter-patters, but I can't stop wanting him to touch me.

"Big," I say the word out loud. The woman who is clearly listening to our conversation stiffens.

The crowd moves, and Jared puts the cactus back on the stand, leaning in again. My heart picks up, but it doesn't go into a frenzy. My body's enjoying the contact with him way too much. When he leans back, he pauses, his gaze flickering over my face. Amusement shines in his eyes like he knows what he's doing to me.

"I want to be with you." My breath catches in my chest after I say the words.

He doesn't have to ask in what way. My nipples press against my dress and feel heavy in my bra. The thoughts of having Jared inside me are all-consuming, and I haven't stopped thinking about having him fully.

A girl brushes against me as people are trying to get past us. I take the lead and tug Jared's hand so we continue to walk. I want him to say something, but he isn't giving anything away, and I wonder if I even said the words out loud.

I focus on my surroundings again. I have no knowledge of ninety-five percent of the plants, but Jared compliments my knowledge of flowers continuously throughout our day. Of the mere five percent that I have some knowledge of, I've gathered from books, Google, and going to our local Garden center. Tom, a horticulturist who works at our local garden center, also has a garden show on my favorite radio station. It's always fun to listen to and is very knowledgeable. I usually listen to Tom every Saturday morning at nine thirty, but I haven't in a while.

We finally come across the waterfall that has been erected in the center of the exhibition. The bottom is full of loose coins. An elderly couple sits eating ice cream opposite us. I lick my lips, my mouth dry from the heat of the day. But we haven't come across a stand that sells water.

"Open your hand."

My attention snaps to Jared. I do slowly, not trusting the grin on his face. "Do you need me to close my eyes?" I ask.

"No." He places some coins in my hands. "Go make some wishes. I'll be back in a moment."

I force a smile and a quick nod as I walk to the waterfall. I swallow another lump in my throat. Every time I'm around him, he either makes me want to burst into tears or touch him in some way.

Every Saturday when we were kids, we would go into town with his friends. He always took me along, even when they protested.

At the Kid's Center, there was a maze of mirrors, and right in the middle was a wishing well. We never had much, but Jared always managed to get a coin for me. Every time we went, I would spend what felt like hours in the maze. I never gave up until I found the wishing well. Once I was there, I made the same wish every time.

I look down at the coins in my hand. I always wished that someone would come and take Jared and me away from Bert and Ronnie. That we would grow up together and be happy.

"I've upset you again."

I squeal, not expecting Jared to be there.

He sits down beside me.

"No, I was only thinking about the wish I always made when we were kids," I say.

He raises an eyebrow. "You made the same wish every time?"

I nod. "Yeah."

"Was it to have your wicked way with me?" Jared grins before reaching over and closing my hand around the coins. The heat of his fingers sears me. "I mean, I can make that wish come true." Jared takes his hand off me but still wears the cheeky smile.

I open my hand and look down at my palm. "I wished that someone would take us away, and we could grow up together and be happy."

There is a long pause, and around us, the sounds press in.

"Well, we found each other, and we are happy." He leans away so he can look at me. "I know I'm happy now that I've found you."

"I'm happy I found you too, Jared."

His warmth and smell surround me as he pulls me into his chest. I don't want to cry. So I focus on the rapid beat of his heart. It pounds heavily against his solid chest.

"I was lost without you." His words and the gentle stroke of his hand down my back have my nerve endings on fire. What is happening to me? These feelings that rush through my body make me feel like breathing him in is the only right thing to do. Like he's my oxygen, my life support, and if I lose him again,

I won't survive. I move out of his arms with reluctance, but I need to answer him.

"Me, too."

He visibly takes in a deep breath, his hands on my arms. I'm not sure if he's aware of his movements. He rubs his hands up and down my arms, causing a frenzy inside me. My thoughts veer off the PG-13 road again, and I know I need to stop them, for a million reasons. One reason is that we're in a very public place, and we've already drawn attention from passersby and the elderly couple.

"Let's make a wish together," I tell Jared. It takes him a moment to respond. He blinks several times, like he's just waking up.

"I mean, don't waste a wish on wanting to have your way with me. I surrender." Jared holds up his arms.

I shake my head and grin, pushing the coin into his palm. He takes it and drops his hands.

"Should we tell each other?" he asks.

I roll my eyes. "No, then the wishes won't come true."

"I know. I'm just teasing." The corner of his mouth quirks up, and he winks.

My stomach tightens, and I focus on the water in front of me. I'm not sure what to wish for. Glancing at Jared, I notice he has his eyes closed and the most serious expression on his face. He flips the coin in and doesn't look away until the water swallows it up.

I wish that Jared's wish comes true. I toss in my own coin, and when I glance up, Jared stands with his hand outstretched.

"Let's get some ice cream."

I take Jared's hand. This time, when his fingers entwine with mine, it doesn't completely scramble my brain. It still sends my pulse racing, but it's my body's reaction to Jared. I'm starting to associate it with elevated heart rate, and my thoughts scattering whenever I am near him.

We are finally close to the ice cream stand that has been specially set up for the exhibit. Jared once again recites the same order we often got. Two scoops of chocolate ice cream with tons of chocolate syrup. It simply would not do to just get one. When he passes me mine, I immediately start eating. We walk through a calmer area of the center. This area is mostly seeds; there aren't many potted plants to see. A few garden sheds fill the floor space, and there are also kiosks with leaflets. It makes me think of my garden at home. Maybe a new shed would look nice. I know if I suggested it to Carl and Evelyn, they would buy it without hesitation. But that doesn't seem fair. I should finish the planting and maybe give the shed a fresh coat of paint. Thinking of the garden has my thoughts turning to Evelyn and Carl. How nice it was the last day I was there with them.

"So, it's been over a week?" I take a large bite of the chocolate flake. Jared is eating the cone, his ice cream gone.

"I was wondering if there's any news about..." The person who shall not be named. I don't want to say Chester's name out loud, and thankfully, I don't have to.

"Are you in a rush to leave me?" Jared tries for a light tone, but he doesn't succeed.

"No, of course not. I just also don't like the idea of him walking around."

Jared doesn't answer, and I hate the stiffness of his shoulders, so I make conversation. "Tell me about something that makes you happy." I start eating the second scoop, not sure how much more I can eat. I hope my change in conversation helps relax Jared.

"Boxing. My trainer, Rex, is really supportive. He's the one who encouraged me to compete. I spent so much time training when I first arrived here. It was an outlet I needed at the time."

That makes sense to me, with how buff Jared is.

"I'm really glad you found boxing." I glance at Jared while taking a lick of my ice cream.

"I'm really glad you're enjoying that ice cream." Jared grins.

"Yeah, it's pretty good," I answer, taking one more lick, but I'm searching for a trash can. I can't eat much more.

A green bin with the letters TRASH engraved in gold gives me a moment to allow my stomach to settle. As I pass, I throw in the ice cream.

"Too much?" Jared asks while his eyes dart to the bin, eyebrows drawn down.

"Yeah. My eyes are bigger than my belly," I tell him.

His mouth curves into a smile. "In your case, it is true. You have big eyes."

People often comment on it when they meet me for the first time—either how white blonde my hair is or how big my eyes are. When Bert or his friends mentioned my eyes or hair, it was said with malice, like I was a freak, so I'm still struggling with the idea that people are complimenting me. It's too engraved in me from my childhood.

"Well... you have dimples," I fire back at Jared to take my mind off things that terrify me.

His dimples are on full display as he laughs gently. "I'm complimenting you, Layla. On your eyes."

"And I'm complimenting you on your dimples," I say, feeling confused.

His hand finds mine as we walk, and he twines our fingers together.

"You sound defensive," Jared says, bringing my attention back to his face.

"Sorry, I'm bad at taking compliments," I admit. We have reached the back wall of the garden display and start to make our way back.

"Well, we have to fix that," he replies. "Every day, I'm going to send you a compliment, and soon, you'll accept them."

I swat at his arm, and his eyes flash with amusement. "Don't start texting me stuff," I say, shaking my head, but deep down, excitement bubbles inside me.

The crowded area we first walked into appears quicker than I expect. Knowing that the day is almost over has me feeling disappointed. I've been enjoying myself. We check out some plants that are two years old; their colors are refreshing. I lose Jared at one stage, spending too long looking at a row of pink clematis vines that have been hung from a massive wall. The display is magical. Other plants sit on the base of the stands. The smell of lavender and cape jasmine fills the air.

After I walk through the area and out into the ornamental section, I can still smell the lavender and Jasmine. It's there that I find Jared sitting on a bench, and I steal the moment to study him. His long legs stretch out in front of him and cross at the ankles. He's watching a stream of people move past him. His large tanned arms are folded, showing off his muscular biceps. I bite my lip as I allow myself to take in his strong jawline, perfect lips, and straight nose. His hands tighten around a bag that's tucked under his arm, almost hidden.

"Excuse me." A woman speaks as she slips by me. Now I wonder how many people saw me blatantly staring at Jared. I'm nearly beside him when his gaze travels across me, leaving a path of heat in its wake.

"I'm not sure where I lost you," I say, just trying to keep the heat at bay. Jared is observing me, his eyes darker. I sit down beside him; it's easier than facing him right now. My emotions are running high.

"Thanks for today."

"It's not over yet." Jared smirks at me now.

He stands, his hand stretched out before me.

"What are we doing next?"

"I was thinking of going back home, and you can try on that dress you got."

"The one that Alex picked out for me?" The one I most certainly won't be wearing. "I'm sure she'd love the thought of me modeling it for you." It's a slip of the tongue, which causes Jared to stop walking. The skin around his mouth tightens. He faces me, and my mouth grows dry. His eyes flash with anger.

"I'm sorry. It was a joke." I quickly try to retract my sarcastic statement, but as Jared shakes his head, I know it's too late. I grow concerned and try to pull my hand out of Jared's, but he won't let mine go. My eyes flicker from his tight grip to his fiery eyes. The world shrinks to just him. Everything around us disappears, even the noise. A tremble enters my lip, and I bite down to stop it.

Rocks fill my stomach, and a haze starts to close in around me.

"Jared." One word and it sounds breathless, terrified. It's mine, and I look away from him, waiting for everything to crash down around him. How many times have I been there at the end of someone's wrath?

Countless.

But never Jared's. Never.

I can't bear the silence. Why isn't he saying anything? This is torture.

"Jared," I say again.

"I'll kill her." Jared's eyes flicker around the crowd that has snapped back into focus. His flaring nostrils and tight fists aren't lost on me. I feel a moment of happiness that his anger isn't directed toward me, but it's short lived.

"No. No, I don't think she meant it. You know, she wasn't thinking about my leg." When I speak, Jared's eyes snap to me, and the anger makes me flinch.

"Don't lie to me. What happened?" The tightness around his eyes and jaw has me considering precisely what to say.

"Nothing. Jesus, it's me. I'm just taking everything too per-sonally."

Jared's face reddens. "What happened?" He speaks through clenched teeth. I don't get to answer as Jared starts walking quickly with his long legs, dragging me along with him. I'm half jogging. I should have kept my mouth closed.

CHAPTER FOURTEEN

JARED

I KNOW THAT LOOK. She's trying to backpedal. I'll fucking kill Alex. I can imagine what they did to Layla, and to hear the pain in her words has me marching to my car from the exhibition center. I release Layla's hand and open the door for her. Once she's in her seat, I close it too hard and the car shakes.

I'm trying to calm down, so I don't get into the car immediately. Instead, I stand outside my door. I don't want her to see me this volatile. She's already half-afraid. I can tell by the way she spoke of Kieran. I never want Layla to be afraid of me. I've done so much bad shit, but I always put her first. Never me.

I take a few more calming breaths before I slide into the driver's seat. My temper hasn't disappeared, and I squeeze the steering wheel. I try to relax my clenched jaw. "You should have told me."

She won't answer as she puts on her seat belt and stares out the window.

I start the car and drive home.

"What are you going to do?" She wedges her hands in between her legs.

I loosen my hold on the steering wheel, and color comes back into my knuckles. "Have a word." The words grind through my teeth.

Layla shifts in her seat. "Just don't fall out over it. She's your friend. I'm sure she didn't mean any offense."

I work a muscle in my jaw. Why is she always so eager to push people's behavior aside?

"Promise me, Jared, that you won't fall out with her."

"Yeah." It wasn't the most convincing promise, but right now it's the best I can do.

"I don't like this at all." She rotates so she's facing me.

"Tough, Layla." I slow down as we approach my home.

"Jared, you've already fallen out with Kieran. Now Alex?"

The gates take longer than usual to open, or maybe it just feels that way.

"Jared." Layla sounds exasperated.

I unbuckle my belt and look at her. "Kieran kissed you. If I could do it all again, I would have kept him under the water." I shift gears and drive up to the house. The garage doors open.

"You don't mean that," Layla whispers.

"I have a boxing session with Rex. Will you be okay here with Kerry and the girls?"

Layla doesn't move. "You know how I feel about unresolved problems. We always sort our differences out before going to bed. No matter how bad things get between us, we sort it out and never let it carry into the next day."

I run my fingers along my lip before speaking. "I suppose, in a way, we weren't like regular kids. Layla, I'm not just going to let this go with Alex."

"Fine." Layla reaches for the door but doesn't get out. "Jared, please."

I sit back in the seat before tilting my head toward her. "We're good, Layla. I promise."

"You promise me you'll remain friends with Alex," Layla pleads.

I look away from her. That should be an answer enough.

"Oh my God, Jared. It's not a big deal."

"Why are you so hell-bent on me being friends with her?" If she had a male friend, I'd lose it completely. Why is she so okay with me being friends with Alex?

"Because she's your friend, and I don't want to be the cause of you falling out. I feel enough has happened since we found each other."

I face her. "None of that is your fault. We can brush things under the carpet all we want. You can stay quiet to keep the peace with Alex, but inside"—I tap her head—"you will have no peace. So I'm just going to have a chat with her."

Layla stretches out her fingers, and her shoulders roll. "Okay."

Relief immediately floods me. She's starting to see that people can't hurt her and get away with it.

"Thank you." She leans in and kisses me softly on the cheek. She quickly pulls away, turns, and gets out of the car. "Thanks again for today," she says, not looking at me. She's out of the garage and disappearing into the house.

Once Layla is out of sight, I allow all the rage to flood back in. A tornado tears through my system, and I'm reversing out of the garage.

***

I pull up at Alex's front door, which is ajar. Noise coming from the state-of-the-art kitchen has me making my way down the hall.

"Mrs. Davis, you are a sight." I pick up a red apple from the oversized fruit bowl.

Mrs. Davis pushes the glasses from her nose, and they dangle from a crystal chain on her chest. She swats my compliment away while wearing a smile. After moving aside her magazine, she walks around the island to me. I accept a kiss on each cheek.

"Jay, you get better looking every day. I can't wait for you to marry my daughter."

I smile while raising both eyebrows. Like fuck I would ever marry Alex. "Speaking of your daughter, is she here?" I glance around the kitchen.

"I'm afraid not." Mrs. Davis releases me from the brief hug.

Perfect.

I take a bite of the apple, then offer my condolences. "I'm sorry about you and Mr. Davis."

Mrs. Davis half smiles. "Whatever do you mean?"

"Alex was very upset about the divorce. It was a real shock to her."

Her laugh is forced. "Divorce? No one is getting divorced. What did Alex say?"

Alex was lying. I'm not surprised. It's just like her to use any tactic possible to get me alone.

"I must have misheard her," I answer, taking another bite of my apple.

Mrs. Davis grips the crystal chain around her neck. "I doubt that. She must be looking for more attention." Miss Davis forgets herself for a moment. Her speaking so freely isn't something I've heard her do before.

When I chomp on the apple, she forces another smile, like she remembers I'm here.

Her phone rings, and she raises a hand while looking at her screen.

"I have to take this."

"No problem."

She answers the call.

With her back to me, I don't linger but make my way to the stairs.

When I reach Alex's room, I've finished my apple and throw the core in her empty velvet wastebasket. Alex's room is the opposite of the house she lives in. Here, she favors the color black. Black bedding, a black leather headboard. The canvas painting behind her bed is all different shades of black. It's angry and interesting. When I asked her about it, she shrugged and said she just wanted a painting.

A wooden ladder to the left takes me to the loft above her bedroom. It looks right down on her bed. Up here is where we often studied—or pretended to anyway. A large white desk, which I'm sure her mother selected, is bare. The only thing that decorates the space is a black lamp.

I open the first drawer to find scraps of paper. I have no idea what I'm looking for. Maybe some dirt on Alex so I can humiliate her like she did Layla. There's nothing here; only a few notes from William about times for her to be at the house. Three of them are clipped together. One was from when we went to a charity event, and one was a request from my father after the shooting. Funny how he dates them all. The third is from the fifteenth of January. I'm not sure what that was for. That was before Layla arrived, and I'm sure I had a competition that day and was gone for the entire weekend.

I leave the loft and do a quick check of her underwear drawer, but there's nothing but her panties and a purple vibrator. When I return downstairs, Mrs. Davis is still talking on the phone. The sound of her raised voice carries into the hallway, and I don't return to the kitchen but leave their home.

So, Alex was lying about her parents' divorce. I didn't think I could really do anything with that information, only call her out on her lie.

I go straight to the gym. The urge to drive home and check on Layla nearly has me turning the car around.

I arrive at the gym and get my pre-packed gym bag out of the trunk. Like always, the gym is empty, and Rex is in his office. I knock on the glass, and he raises his head. I open the door, but I don't enter.

"When I fought in that competition in Inishmore, was that in January?" I ask.

Rex squeezes the bridge of his nose before folding his arms across his chest. "I think so. Why?"

"No reason. Just curious." I tap the doorframe.

"Are you thinking of fighting again?" Hope fills his voice.

I hate to be the one to kill that notion. "I'm still thinking about it," I lie before leaving his office and getting ready to practice.

Rex is waiting for me by the ring when I come out onto the gym floor. I crack my neck from side to side.

Rex is quiet as he wraps my hands. I zone in on the beat of the music that pumps out from the overhead speakers.

"That fight down in Inishmore was in January." Rex tugs on my gloves. "It was the weekend of the fifteenth. I looked it up for you."

"Thanks." Why did my father request to see Alex that day? To talk about me, no doubt.

I'm ready to get into the ring when Rex grips both of my gloved hands, stopping me from walking away.

I knew something was bothering him with his silence, and now I'm about to find out. "You're a good kid, Jay. I don't want to see you getting hurt." He releases my hands.

"Why would I get hurt?" I smash my gloved hands together and smirk, trying to lighten the mood. "I mean, I can take care of myself, thanks to you."

"Warren O'Reagan is bad news."

I exhale and stop smirking. "Not this again." I climb into the ring, and Rex takes a moment before he joins me with the boxing pads in his hands.

"Yes, this again. That kid..."

I strike hard, but Rex holds still.

"He's angry, and angry people..."

I strike harder, and Rex moves back slightly.

"Are dangerous people." Rex drops his hands.

I nearly hit him but pull back at the last second. "What the fuck, Rex? I nearly hit you!"

Rex isn't fazed at all and takes a step closer to me. "I'm trying to look out for you."

"I don't need anyone looking out for me." I've spent my whole life taking care of myself. I don't need someone else.

Rex holds up his padded hands. "Fine, Jay. If you ever need me, I'm here."

Fuck's sake, why did he have to get like this? "I know," I tell him. I take a swing for the pad, and Rex says no more about Warren.

I'm soaked by the time we finish training, and some of my anger toward Alex is gone. Rex unwraps my hands, and I hit the shower.

He's back in the office when I leave. I salute him, and he responds with a jerk of his head. I leave the gym. The light outside is bright. Removing my phone, I think of ringing home to check on Layla, but I pause.

Words are displayed across my car windshield. I glance around the area, but the only vehicle that's here is Rex's pickup truck. The closer I get, the tighter my fists grow.

"RIP" is sprayed in thick black letters.

I drop my gym bag, unzip it, and grab my workout top while dialing home.

William answers on the first ring as I run my top along the glass.

"Is Layla there?"

I scrub harder, but the letters won't come off. I turn as Rex comes out the main door. He must have seen me on CCTV.

"Yes, Master Jay. She's in her quarters with Kerry."

"Go check, William," I say as I drop my top back into my gym bag.

Rex stands beside me, and his jaw twitches as he reads the letters on my windshield.

"One moment, Master Jay."

I look around the area and walk toward the bushes. Some rocks are placed throughout the undergrowth. I hoist the largest one.

"What are you doing?" Rex asks as I come back to the car with the rock.

"Yes, Master Jay. Layla is in her quarters. I'm looking at her right now. Shall I put her on..."

I hang up and push the phone into my pocket before launching the rock at my windshield. The impact is instant, and the glass splinters and cracks, the center caving in on itself.

"Are you going to explain to me why you did that?" Rex folds his arms across his chest.

"It's a warning." I pick up my gym bag.

"I can see that, Jay." Rex's voice carries a note of irritation.

I face him while slinging my bag over my shoulder. "Can you give me a lift home?"

He keeps his arms folded.

"I'll tell you everything on the way."

That has him unfolding his arms. "Let me grab my keys."

I wait outside as he heads back into the building.

I ring the breakdown service to pick up the car and fix the windshield. I leave the keys on the front tire. I'm finished with the call when Rex returns with his car.

I throw my bag in his open trunk before climbing in.

"My girlfriend, Layla, was shot."

"When? Why didn't you say anything?"

Is that hurt I see in his gaze? "I don't talk about her," I admit. Layla isn't something I've discussed before, so it's like all I know is to keep everything about her to myself.

"Is she okay?" Rex's voice lowers.

"Yeah, but the guy who shot her"—I point over at my car—"isn't finished yet."

Rex follows my stare to my car. "Can I ask why someone wants to kill your girlfriend?"

No.

"Retaliation toward me."

"You've been mixing with some bad people, Jay." Rex leans on the steering wheel. This is a lot for him to take in.

"This has got nothing to do with Warren." I defend him straight away, seeing where this conversation is going.

Rex nods before starting the Jeep. "So why did I just watch you smash your windshield?"

"I don't want Layla upset," I admit. "She ended up in a coma and had some memory loss, but recently she remembers who shot her."

"But you knew him? So the Gardaí can deal with this."

I take out my phone and check the time. It's nearly six in the evening. "At the time, she didn't remember," I repeat.

Rex gives a laugh. "I see, and you were hoping it would remain that way."

I glance at him.

"What did you do, Jay?"

"I beat up their gang leader."

Rex shakes his head. "Never use your skills like that." Disappointment is heavy in his words.

"Yeah, I fucked up. Take a left here," I instruct, realizing that Rex doesn't know where I live, and we're out of the main part of the town.

"I'll go to the Gardaí."

"Good."

Silence follows, and the only words exchanged are me giving instructions to Rex.

We pull up at the gates. "I'll walk from here." I don't need my father to see Rex. I'm sure that would set him off.

I get out, and Rex rolls down the window. "If you need me, Jay, you know where I am."

I look away before getting my bag out of the trunk. "Thanks for the lift," I call over my shoulder before ringing the gates, and they open.

I had no luck finding Chester, so I think going public will flush him out. I want him dead.

William materializes in the hallway. "Good evening, Master Jay. Your food is in your room, and Miss Masters is in her quarters."

"Thank you, William," I say while handing him my gym bag. I don't make my way to my room. Instead, I go to the security hut that's stationed in the back of the property. It's not somewhere I've been before, and when I open the door, the two men who are having a chat stand up. The first nearly sloshes his tea across his knee as he rises, dropping a chocolate digestive onto his desk. He fixes his tie. "Master Jay."

"How far back do we keep footage?" I ask.

It takes him a moment to recover. "A full year."

I have no idea why we would. "Can you get me the tapes for the fifteenth of January?"

He swings into action. The other guy stands close to the door.

"Take a break," I tell him and he leaves, closing the door behind us.

There must be twelve televisions in the room—a bit overkill if you ask me. "This is a lot of surveillance," I say, looking around the room.

"Your father wanted the best, Master Jay."

I lean in behind the security guard. He glances at me but gets back to work.

"Well, I'd say you did a piss-poor job. People seem to be able to waltz in and out of here. Like the day of the shooting."

He tries to turn his chair, but I grip the back of it. "Do your job."

He goes back to looking through records. "The day of the shooting, someone had cut the cameras, Master Jay."

His snooty tone has me grinning at the back of his head. That one mistake cost me dearly. "Did you not look into the fault?" I ask. I had cut the power from the main board, but they must have known that.

"We were told it was better to turn a blind eye."

I don't have to ask who said it. My father. So he'd known Layla was here that night, even before the shooting. "By who?" I still need it clarified.

"Your father, Master Jay."

"What about my mother? How did she get in so easily?" I stare at the screen as he continues to search.

"I can look into it for you."

"You do that." I lean in closer as he opens a file.

"Here we are."

"Take a break," I say, and he gets out of his chair right before I slide into it.

I stay with the camera on the front door and fast forward it throughout the day. It takes a few more minutes before Alex arrives. I sit closer to the screen to see where she reappears. In the hallway downstairs. She reappears in my father's study. Alex walks along the bookshelves, and he appears. There's no audio, so I have no idea what's being said. A very pointless search.

I'm ready to turn it off when Alex leans into my father and kisses him.

What the fuck?

I must be mistaken. Any uncertainty I have vanishes as she slowly drops to her knees and starts to give my father a blow job.

CHAPTER FIFTEEN

LAYLA

AFTER TAKING A BATH and changing into another dress, this one baby pink, I sit down for my food at the table that's nestled between the windows. Kerry hasn't left my bedroom, and Amanda arrives back in. Amanda tidies the area while Kerry brushes my hair. I'm glad I don't have to wear my sling anymore. I can move my arm more, but brushing my hair won't be easy.

It's been hours since Jared dropped me off, and when he enters my room, there's a clear shift in the air.

He juts his chin toward me and lowers his eyebrows. "You okay?"

The sandwich I've been eating feels lodged in my throat. "What's wrong?" I get up, and Kerry steps away from me.

Jared holds up his hands. "Nothing."

Everything.

"Can you give us the room?" Jared addresses Kerry and Amanda.

"Yes, Master Jay." Kerry holds out her arm toward Amanda to hurry her up. Amanda places the clothes she was holding onto the bed, and within seconds, the bedroom door closes, and it's just Jared and me. I get up as Jared steps closer to me, and the way he's looking at me makes me unbalanced.

"I love you, Layla." Jared touches my face.

"I know. I love you too." Fear finds its way into my words. "What's going on?"

Jared touches his lips against mine before releasing me. "We need to go to the Gardaí about Chester. He left another message, and I'm realizing he won't be going away."

My legs should buckle; my body should sag. I should be overwhelmed with relief, but I'm not. Instead, I have this feeling of being smothered, and it overshadows everything else as I stagger away from Jared.

"But we lied. We can't just change our minds. They'll know."

"No, they won't," Jared reasons. "You had memory loss. You just got your memory back."

I can sense the edges of hysteria at the thoughts of going to the Gardaí after lying.

"You never lied to them, Layla. At the time you gave your statement, you didn't know." Jared speaks as if he read my mind.

"What about you? Are you okay with lying?"

Jared's smile is quick, and it drips with a silent story of hurt and pain. "Yeah, I'm good with lying to them."

My stomach coils as if I've swallowed something poisonous. I turn to try to find some of my footing, but Jared's arms circle me, and I'm against his solid chest.

"When we were kids, I rang them to help us," Jared whispers in my ear. "And they didn't." His voice is low, but his words are loud. Hot pain burns a path right down to my tattered soul. "I rang them so many times when he was—"

I turn in Jared's arms, and he lets me. I'm expecting to see a pair of dark eyes filled with unshed tears, but the only thing Jared's gaze is filled with is hardness. His arms drop to my waist, and I rest my hands on his chest. "So I'm okay with lying to them, Layla."

My anger is hanging on by a thread, and it snaps as I lean against Jared's chest. His heart thrashes wildly under my ear.

"I love you," I say on a whoosh of expelled air.

Jared presses a kiss to the crown of my head. "I love all of you."

When I glance up at Jared, his eyes are still hard. I reach up and touch his brow, tracing it with my finger. "Smile for me, Jared." My words are soaked in the pain that our past has coated us in.

His lips lift slightly.

"That's the best you can do for me?" I keep my hand over his pounding heart.

He focuses over my head, and when he glances back, his dimples make an appearance. I reach up on the tip of my toes and press a kiss to his lips. "Once we do this, I'll need to tell Evelyn and Carl." My shoulders sag at the thoughts of the conversation with Evelyn and Carl.

Jared releases me. "Okay. Are you ready to go now?"

"Yeah, let me grab my shoes." I find my tennis shoes and grab my bag and denim jacket. Jared waits patiently, and when I turn with everything in my hand, he stops me from leaving. His long fingers circle my wrist.

"I'll be with you every step of the way."

My heart *thump, thump, thumps* in my chest. "I know."

***

Jared keeps to his word and never leaves my side through the two-hour ordeal at the Gardaí station. By the time he drops me off at Carl and Evelyn's, I'm emotionally spent.

I let myself in with my own key, and Jared doesn't leave until I close the door and lean against it. I listen as his car pulls away, and my body is ready to sag. I don't want to crash in the hall. I take the stairs two at a time, not being able to reach my room quickly enough.

"What happened?" Evelyn stands on the landing with a pile of clean clothes in her arms. Her brows knit together as she moves toward me. I try to focus on the swish of her full-length tan skirt to stop the harrowing feeling that's consuming every inch of my fiber.

"Layla?" she questions, drawing me to her worried gaze. The tightening of her eyes should have been a warning for me to put her mind at rest, but I don't. Instead, I let the whole day's emotions pour from me. My tears have Evelyn dropping the clothes and embracing me, which makes me cry harder.

"Shh. It's okay, sweetheart." Evelyn's hand runs up and down my back in a soothing rhythm, but it doesn't stop the onslaught of emotions that pour from me. Today, everything that I've kept tucked away comes crashing down.

"What happened?" The strength in Evelyn's voice isn't the therapist I'm used to. It's more of what I imagine a fierce mother would sound like.

"You'll hate me, and I wouldn't blame you." I sniffle.

"What happened?"

I stiffen but don't turn at Carl's voice. I plead with Evelyn with my eyes.

"Just girl talk. It's fine." Evelyn gives a smile to Carl over my head. I don't want her to lie to him, but I appreciate it more than she will ever know. Carl would only get mad at Jared, and that's the last thing I want.

"I'll be downstairs," Carl says reluctantly. The stairs creak under his weight as he descends the stairs.

I wait alone with Evelyn, who wants an explanation. She releases me, and we walk to the room that we set up for meditation and where I do most of my therapy with Evelyn. It's a room I don't associate with pain and hurt, even though I've poured my heart and soul out in this room. No. It's a room of healing and love for me.

I focus on my surroundings to ground myself. The room is scarcely furnished, but that's the point. It isn't a big room, but it feels spacious. The clever arrangement of the furniture and the use of light colors make it appear large. The walls are painted in a simple magnolia, while the wooden floor is glossed over in white paint. I curl up in my hanging chair that Carl had hung from the ceiling. The large circle is a safe space for me, a warm cocoon where Bert or Ronnie can't get me. Evelyn sits across from me on a large wicker chair that has several floral throws strewn across the back.

I slip off my shoes and let them fall on the shaggy cream rug that covers most of the wooden floor before tucking my bare feet under me. Evelyn lights her incense that sits on a wicker-style table. I always love the smell and find it relaxes me, but not today.

"I could never hate you, Layla." Evelyn's smile is as soft as fresh whipped cream, making me want to smile too. Her kindness always steals a bit of my fear at times like this.

"I know who shot me. I lied about it."

She shifts in her seat, moving forward. Her fingers tap her leg, and she nods several times. "Who?"

Who doesn't really matter. "Chester. I babysat for his girlfriend a few nights before the shooting, and we had words. He wasn't happy I was minding his child."

Evelyn sits forward. "Do you think he shot you because of that?"

Everything feels tight: my dress, my chest, the lies. Lies that won't stop. "No, I don't. I think it was a coincidence that I met him before he robbed Jared's home and shot me." I try to find some resolve before I shatter. Tears make paths down my cheeks. "I'm sorry I lied."

"Did you lie because you were afraid?"

I nod. It's easier than using my words.

"I have a confession," Evelyn says as she reaches to pick up the lighter that she used to light the incense. "I didn't like Jared. I never wanted you to find him."

Her words carve more pain into me, and I find myself pulling my floral cushion to my chest. I blink several times. I kind of knew this, but her saying it really brings it home. "But," she continues, "I tracked him down years ago. I've known where he was all this time."

A bitter taste pools in my mouth. The gash that my past carved into my soul reopens all over again.

Evelyn's eyes glaze with unshed tears. "I keep waiting for you to fully blossom in your life, but I knew something was holding you back. So..." The smile she wears rips a strip of anger from me. She tilts her head and blinks, tears falling. "I packed up our lives and dropped you across Ireland so you could hopefully find your peace."

Evelyn wipes her face with both hands before rubbing them together. "Ever since we arrived here, I've kept waiting for you to come alive again." She swallows all her tears. "You do, Layla. You come alive around Jared, and I'm so sorry I kept you from him all that time."

Her words cause tears to pour soundlessly down my face. She's telling me what I already knew, what I've been trying to explain. We aren't unhealthy together. I swipe the tears away.

"I'm sorry I've been so hard on him. I'm sorry I've been so hard on you." She holds her head high, trying to hide the fact that her apology is taking far more out of her than she's willing to admit.

She lied to me. I lied to her. We both did it to protect the other, yet all we seem to have done is cause each other pain.

"Layla." Evelyn sits forward, joining her hands together. "I was afraid I might have made the wrong judgment call to bring you here. I was afraid it would open new wounds too widely."

"Since I've had Jared back in my life, I realize what I've always been missing. Him." The confession makes my heart squeeze. I pick at my nails. "He's the same person." I don't look up at Evelyn. I don't like how those words make me feel. "He's hiding something from me."

"Okay, let's start with what you think he could be hiding." Evelyn is now very much in therapist mode, and I shift slightly, wondering if I really want to go down this road with her. But

I need to. I can't let it keep spinning around in my mind. And frankly, I have no one else to talk to.

"He carries a lot of anger." I chew my lip.

"Did you talk to Jared about it?" Evelyn tilts her head, and I suppress a smile. It's a tell that she's uncomfortable with what I'm saying, but she's trying to stay in the moment.

"He's never angry toward me." I put her mind at rest before I continue. "He's angry at everyone else." I let my legs hang out of the chair.

"He's violent at times." My words are low as I think of Kieran. I hate telling Evelyn, but I can't seem to let that knowledge go.

"Layla. I have raised you for the last seven years of your life. You are my *daughter*, and I can see it in your eyes that something has happened. So you're going to tell me the *truth*." Evelyn's tone is fierce, and so much of that sentence has my head spinning.

She just called me her daughter.

"I kissed Kieran and Jared saw it. He attacked Kieran," I admit.

A slow smile transforms Evelyn's face. "He was jealous. Boys fight."

I want to tell her she wasn't there. She didn't see how he held Kieran under the water, or how he tried to buy a gun to shoot Bert. Jesus, the more I think about it, the more I realize that telling her all this is madness.

"Yeah, you're probably right." Outside the window, the sky has turned a deep crimson color, and I focus on the rays that scatter across the horizon from the setting sun. Thinking of Bert makes me think of Nelson. "I wish I had time with Nelson before he died. I wish I had gotten to talk to him." I look back at Evelyn.

Her eyes flash with knowledge before she speaks. "We actually got more word about Nelson. I was able to dig around, and we found out his cause of death."

I grip my foot and pull it up onto the chair, waiting.

"I'm so sorry, Layla. Nelson took his own life."

The room spirals, and my chest constricts as I repeat Evelyn's words. "Nelson took his own life."

"I'm afraid so, sweetheart." Evelyn nods several times.

Pain leaks from my eyes faster than I can think. "He was, what?" I blink but my vision doesn't clear as I produce more tears at a brutal rate. "Eighteen, Nineteen?"

"I'm not sure, love."

I blink Evelyn into focus. "Why?"

Evelyn shrugs, her fingers tightening on the lighter. "No one knows."

All I can think is: I need to tell Jared.

We sit in silence for a long time, and I get lost in a pool of heartache and pain. The sky darkens when Evelyn finally speaks.

"How are you feeling?" Her voice snaps me back to the present.

"It's so weird. You know"—I frown at my own thoughts—"it makes sense. Even as a kid, Nelson always held such... anger, darkness, hurt." A chill slides across my skin and a whisper niggles at me. *Nelson isn't the only one who harbored such emotions.*

"It's a pity to see a young life taken. Grieve for him, Layla, but don't get swallowed up in his pain."

I nod. I have a habit of doing just that. "I won't."

My phone buzzes in my bag, and I don't need to look to know who it is. I get off the chair and rummage through my purse.

"I'll be out in a minute," I say to Jared before ending the call and facing Evelyn.

She rises and holds out her arms. "I'm so proud of you."

I step into her embrace, and her warmth seeps into my soul. The heaviness I feel starts to lift, and I forgot how powerful Evelyn's hugs are. "I love you, Evelyn."

"I love you too, Layla."

I break the embrace. "Once Chester is arrested, I'll come home."

"Carl and I would really like that." Evelyn's eyes burn so brightly with happiness, and I give her one final hug before putting on my shoes and gathering my bag and jacket, and some strength. This will be all over soon, I tell myself.

CHAPTER SIXTEEN

JARED

"Where are the paintings?" my father shouts through the phone.

I lift my head and glance up at Layla's window before answering him. "Safe." My one word has him growling through the phone.

"Jay, this is no time for your smartness. Where are they?"

I'm tempted to hang up, when I see movement close to the front door. I just rang Layla to tell her I'm outside.

I look at the phone. "Layla remembers who shot her, so we reported it to the Gardaí like good citizens. So the paintings are in their rightful place."

I had to call in another favor with Warren O'Reagan. He hasn't told me what it will cost, but I'm sure it won't be cheap. He had his men move the paintings into Chester's home before I took Layla to the Gardaí station.

"I'm sure by now Chester has been arrested, and we will be receiving a phone call to say our artwork has been recovered."

My father breathes heavily. "I'll speak to you when you get home." He has absolutely no gratitude for what I've done.

Layla steps out of Evelyn and Carl's house, and she wraps her arms around her waist.

"Yeah, see you then." I hang up. I have no intention of going home. The closer Layla gets to my car, the clearer she becomes. She's been crying. Layla doesn't look at me as she walks around the car and gets in. Evelyn stands at the door and waves. I don't wave back until I know what's happened and why Layla was crying.

"What happened? Did she upset you?"

Layla's gaze is drawn to Evelyn, and her hand rises as she gives a small wave. "No."

I turn the keys in the ignition and pull away from Layla's home.

"She knew where you were all this time." Layla's voice hitches with upset. "She always knew," Layla repeats.

I also knew this. My father already told me. When I don't answer, Layla's eyes widen.

"Why aren't you saying anything? I thought you would be cursing her?"

Her analysis is fair. "My father told me when you first arrived that Evelyn was aware of where I lived. I just didn't believe it."

"You didn't think to tell me?"

The sensation that rises inside me has me gripping my hands on the steering wheel. "My father lies a lot, so I didn't know what to believe."

Layla lets out a long breath and slumps lower in the seat. "I told her about Chester as well. So, no more secrets."

When my gaze meets Layla's, I have this need to know what she isn't saying. It scorches itself on my skin; it's angry.

I push it aside and focus on driving. "I want to show you something," I say.

Layla sits up straight and grips the overhead handle.

We arrive in town, which is quiet at this hour of the night. Nervousness isn't an emotion I'm accustomed to, but that's what has me dragging my hands through my hair several times. I do it enough to garner Layla's attention. She raises a brow.

"Are you okay?" She turns in her seat.

"Yes. Stop worrying," I say and it's funny how sure and confident I sound, when really my insides churn uncomfortably.

I approach the empty gym and pull up close to the door. I take out the set of keys that Rex gave me.

"A gym?" Layla dips her head and stares out the windshield.

"Come on." I get out of the car, and Layla does the same.

I open the front door and lock it behind us. Flicking on all the overhead lights, Layla looks at me shyly over her shoulder, and automatically, I reach out and take her hand.

"This is where I practice with Rex." My heart thumps rapidly in my chest. It's not a big deal. It *shouldn't* be a big deal, but really, it is. It's a part of me that I've never shared with anyone I've cared for, and I want to share it with Layla.

I let my fingers leave the safety of Layla's hand and slide my fingers up her wrist, stopping on her rapid heartbeat.

My fingers trail from her wrist, and I walk toward the ring. I get in it and turn so I'm facing Layla. "This is where the magic happens." I grin.

She smiles.

Layla tucks her hands behind her back, and I'm waiting for her to walk to me, but she makes her way to a large glass case instead. "I'm assuming some of these trophies are yours?"

The teasing in her voice has me jumping down from the ring. The moment my feet touch the ground, she glances at me. I love how she swallows as I walk toward her. She makes me feel far more powerful than I am. I don't stand beside her but stop right behind her and inhale her scent.

"A few," I say and brush her hair over one shoulder. I meet her gaze in the glass.

"I don't think I could watch you getting hit." She chews her lip.

I laugh and she turns. I have to take a step back to give her some room. "It's a good thing, then, that I don't get hit."

"Cocky." She's fighting a grin.

I take her hand and lead her to the boxing area. "I'll show you how skilled I am." I grip her waist and lift her until she's standing on the edge of the ring. I climb up and hold the rope so she can enter.

"It's so much bigger when you're up here." Layla walks around.

"Everyone says that."

Layla tuts and heat scorches her cheeks.

I dance slowly from foot to foot. The action is automatic once I enter a ring. "When I'm here, everything fades away. It's only me and Rex. Or me and my opponent. Nothing else."

Layla's fingers flutter rapidly along the sides of her pink dress as she nods. "Like me with gardening."

I stop shifting from foot to foot. "Like you with gardening," I repeat before walking to her and capturing her chin in my hand.

"Teach me some moves." Layla's gaze dances along my mouth.

I release her. "I won't go easy on you," I warn as I step back.

Her laugh is infectious and twists my gut. Fuck me, she's gorgeous. "I won't go easy on you either."

"Let's dance, Layla Masters." I can't stop the stupid smile that crosses my face as I bounce on my feet and hold my fists close to my face.

Layla mimics my actions, and she looks so fucking cute. I shift closer to her, and she strikes. Her small fists impact my arm.

"Easy there, tiger," I say.

She barks a laugh and drops her hands. "Shut up. I'm not made of muscle like some people."

I drop my hands from my face. "I'll gladly show you all my muscles."

Her eyes dance with excitement, and I clear the space between us, done playing. I capture her mouth with mine. Her lips are soft and warm, and I devour her. My cock grows, and I wrap an arm around Layla's waist, dragging her small frame against mine. Her breath hitches. My hand easily slides down until I cup her perfectly round ass. Her hands grip my shoulders, and I lift her, wanting her closer. She automatically wraps her legs around my waist as I push my tongue deeper into her mouth. I move us to the padded corner of the ring. I let her slide down so I can press my cock against her core.

"I want you to touch me." Layla arches her body impatiently against mine. My blood roars in my ears, and I'm hanging on by a thread. It breaks as I trail my fingers under her dress. She holds her breath at the contact and exhales loudly as I push her panties aside and slide my fingers slowly between her folds.

Layla's hands dig into my shoulders, and she tries to bury her head in my chest.

"Look at me."

She does as I remove my finger before pushing it inside her again. I gather some of her wetness and withdraw my finger only to rub it along her clit in long, tantalizing strides. My cock presses painfully against my jeans. I lean my forehead against Layla's as I withdraw my fingers and fix her dress back into place.

As much as I want Layla right now, I don't want to give Rex a show.

"I don't want you to stop." The confession from Layla's pretty mouth tests my willpower.

"I don't want to stop either." I bring my wet fingers to my mouth and taste the sweetness of Layla.

Her eyes widen, and the excitement I recognize in her gaze has me taking her hand. "Let's go home."

She doesn't answer, but her fingers tighten around my hand. I turn off all the lights and lock up before we leave.

The moment we're in the car, I can't help myself as I reach out and grip Layla by the back of the neck, dragging her to me.

"I want to fuck you." I press a kiss between each word.

Layla's breath grows harsh. "I want that too."

I turn the ignition and try to keep to the speed limit.

Layla chews on her bottom lip, and I don't want to give her time to think. I don't want her to change her mind. I run my hand under her dress. Her legs part easily for me, and she shimmies down on the seat, giving me access to her folds.

My finger sinks inside her, and her pussy coils tightly around my fingers. My cock twitches. I extract my finger to run the wetness along her folds before pushing two fingers inside her.

She's gripping the door, and I'm contemplating pulling over and taking her here and now. I would, I fucking would, only I remind myself she's a virgin.

When I extract my hand to shift gears, I press the two fingers that had been buried in her against my lips.

"You taste so sweet." Just like I knew she would.

Layla appears dazed as she sits up and fixes her dress. The gates to my home appear, and this time when I glance at Layla, the nerves are back as she wrings her hands repeatedly in her lap.

I try to grapple for control as I pull into the garage. "We don't have to have sex, Layla."

I stop the car and turn it off.

Layla makes no reply at first. "I want to." Her soft reply has me looking at her.

"Good." Because I didn't think I could deliver on the no-sex part.

Layla gets out first, and I fix my erection before getting out and following her into the house. I take her hand automatically and steer her toward my room.

The intensity to have Layla rises rapidly as I get my bedroom door open. I rotate the key once she's in and turn toward her.

She surprises me when she springs forward and slams her mouth on mine. I don't need a second longer to respond, pulling her small body harshly against mine.

I kiss her back as I guide us to the bed. I lie her down, her blonde hair sprawling around her head like a halo. I step back because I've envisioned this a million time. "You look just like I pictured you would," I admit.

I reach down and run my hands up Layla's bare legs and grip her panties as I drag them down slowly. I pull off her tennis shoes and socks, then toss them so they join her panties on the floor.

"Are you sure about this?" I ask for the final time.

She swallows but nods. "Yes, I want this."

I crawl onto the bed and bury my head between her legs. Licking her juices from my fingers was nice, but drinking from the source has my hard-on painfully pushing against my jeans. I reach down and open my belt and jeans, trying to give my cock some relief. My tongue slides between her folds, and I lap up her wetness.

She's ready for me. Coming up, I take both of Layla's hands and sit her up so I can pull the dress over her head. Once her bra is off, I throw her clothes on the floor. She tries to cover herself up.

"Don't. You're perfect." I get off the bed, and she obediently places her hands along her side. "Perfection."

Every curve, every freckle on her stomach, the scar on her leg—it's all perfect. It's all Layla.

I pull off my shirt and love when Layla swallows. My jeans and boxers come next, and my cock rages.

I take the strip of condoms from the drawer and rip one open.

"Spread your legs for me," I command as I roll on the condom with a clenched jaw. I want to bury myself inside her, but I know I need to pace myself. She's a virgin.

Once again, Layla does as I ask and spreads her legs. I get back up on the bed and stroke my erection. Her body tenses, and I reach out and run my hand along her stomach, which she sucks in on impact.

"You need to relax," I say, though I know the words are pointless.

I direct my cock to her entrance, and it takes every ounce of resilience not to slam myself inside her. I inch in and allow my body to lower slightly. With my hands on either side of her head, I focus on her face. I don't want to miss one second of taking her virginity. Layla was made just for me.

She rears her head, trying to press her lips against mine, but I don't allow it. "I want to watch you."

I slide a little deeper, her pussy painfully tight around my cock, and Layla tries to press her legs together, but that's not possible as I shift my thighs from side to side, stopping her and pushing my cock a little deeper.

Discomfort on her tightening features has me pulling out slightly before moving back in just a bit. I try to keep the rhythm, and soon it pays off as Layla groans in pleasure. I move slightly faster but not deeper. Layla's hands grip the bedding beneath her, and her head lolls to the side in pleasure. When her eyes flutter closed, I'm ready to tell her to look at me, but she does on her own. I push a bit deeper, wanting to fill every single inch of her sweet, perfect pussy.

"Oh, God." Her groan has my control slipping, and I propel further into her. Her hiss gives me back some of that control, and I slip a bit back out but keep a steady pace for her.

Her breasts swell under my chest; her nipples are hard and brush against me. My balls are full as I struggle to keep control. The thought of pulling out crosses my mind until she groans again in pleasure.

I give in and push all the way in. Her body stills, and her hands slam down on my shoulders. I quickly cover her mouth with mine and pull out only to fill her again. It takes a few strokes before she starts to relax under me. Her fingers don't dig as painfully into my shoulder, and she lets me slip my tongue into her mouth as I move faster. It's not enough for me, but I think I've taken enough from her.

Breaking the kiss, I continue the steady pace, and her eyes widen before her head thrashes to the side. I watch as Layla reaches a height, her hands digging into my shoulders before she comes all over my cock.

CHAPTER SEVENTEEN

LAYLA

I'M NO LONGER A virgin.

"Did you come?" I ask breathlessly. Jared is still inside me. The strain on his face tells me he didn't, which disappoints me.

"What I witnessed was better than coming." He presses a soft kiss to my lips before he pulls out of me with such gentleness. I'm still sore and bite down on my lip so I don't hiss. He's watching me too carefully. "You will be sore for a few days."

I'm tempted to cover myself, but I don't. Jared rolls the condom off his very large cock, which I can't believe fit inside me, and leaves to dispose of it in the bathroom. I sit up on my elbows and marvel at how perfect every single inch of him is.

He's naked apart from the key that dangles around his neck. When he's out of sight, I sit up and pull the blanket around my naked and sore body. Everything about this was perfect. For such a large guy, he was so tender, so careful, so open.

Jared steps out of the bathroom. He's pulled on a pair of sweatpants, but I can still appreciate him bare chested.

I can see his dimples are out as he leans against the doorframe, smiling at me.

It's hard to stay still under his scrutiny.

"I'll have to marry you now." His words are said so offhandedly.

Only for his smile, I would think he was serious. "And why is that, Master Jay?"

He leaves the doorframe quickly and marches toward me. The bed dips under his weight. "Don't 'Master Jay' me." He grabs my waist, and I'm rolling backward on the bed until I'm under Jared. "I've taken your virginity, so I think it's best we get married."

This time, he isn't smiling. I'm waiting for him to laugh or tell me he's joking, but he doesn't.

"I don't think it works that way, Jared."

He clears his throat and sits up, giving me some space. "What if it did? Would you say yes?"

"I'm nineteen." That's the best answer I can give him. The idea of marrying Jared elates me, but we're too young, even if at times I feel like I've lived several lives in my short time on earth.

He's not satisfied; his mouth forms a thin line before he smiles. "It doesn't matter. You're mine no matter what. It's only a matter of time before I marry you." He steals a kiss and some of my breath, and sanity flees with it.

Having Jared forever is a dream come true.

He's watching me, and a sudden explosion of love erupts and takes over everything. "God, I love you."

His eyes are light, like they hold the foundations of what life truly is, the fundamentals of what makes us human. It boils down to the one thing always: Love.

"I love you, Layla." He moves closer. His fingers circle my ankle before he opens them and runs them along my calf. They dance across my scar; his touch stitches my wound a little tighter.

His gaze flashes with a touch of anger before it vanishes, and his fingers skim higher. I reach out and press my hand over his chest. I love the feel of it under my touch.

My fingers shift until I pick up the key. He freezes, and my gaze snaps to him as I drop the key. "Sorry."

He clears his throat while his brows drag down. "No, it's only a key."

I pick the key back up. "It's pretty." I smile at him before focusing on the small carvings. "What does it open? A safe?"

"My heart."

I laugh and drop the key before pressing my hand against his racing heart. I shift closer and lean in. Jared licks his bottom lip, and I capture his tongue before he pulls it back into his mouth. A knock on the door has us separating.

"I'll get rid of them." Jared presses a kiss to my forehead before getting off the bed. I tug the blankets tighter around me.

Jared doesn't open the door fully. "William."

"Master Jay." William's voice floats into the room. Jared closes the door and turns, holding a piece of paper, which he opens.

"It's good news." He finishes reading before walking back to me. "Chester has been arrested."

"That's fantastic." My shoulder burns at the reminder, and I reach up and touch the place where I was shot.

Jared rejoins me on the bed. "You don't have to worry anymore."

"Neither do you," I say because I'm not seeing the joy I feel displayed on Jared's features. He's still tense.

"Our artwork was recovered too," he adds.

"That's good, right?"

Jared forces a smile, but it's all wrong on his handsome face. "Of course, Layla."

I reach out and take his hand in mine. "Then why don't you look happy?" I tilt my head as I ask.

"I'll be happy when he's rotting behind bars."

I agree with Jared on this. I hope I never hear Chester's name again. "Evelyn and Carl will be so happy. I can go home soon." Even as I say it, I don't feel the excitement the words should bring me.

"Home?" Jared's eyes pool with darkness.

Adrenaline shoots through my body, and I have no idea what to do with it. I slide off the bed, only for Jared to stop me. His arm circles my waist, and he pulls me back into his chest. "Maybe after the court case."

We both know there's no need for me to stay here any longer. I glance down at Jared's hand as it rests on my abdomen. "That makes sense."

Jared brushes a kiss to my cheek before pressing his face to mine. "Perfect sense."

I grin, but my smile soon dwindles as I think of Evelyn's excitement to have me home. That leads my mind to Nelson. I still haven't told Jared about how Nelson died.

It doesn't feel like the right time, but I'm not sure there ever will be a right time.

"I found out how Nelson died." I place my hand over Jared's. My focus is on the black ink tattoo on his wrist.

I'm waiting for him to ask me how, but when he doesn't, I give in. "He took his own life." Anger pools heavily in my mouth, and when I swallow, it settles with an empty thud in the pit of my stomach.

"This is when I need you to say something."

Jared presses a brash kiss to my cheek, then he releases me and he's off the bed. I spin, trying to understand what's going on.

"What do you want me to say?" He opens a drawer and pulls out a dark T-shirt before putting it on.

Every muscle in my body tightens to a breaking point. "Anything." I squeeze between my numb lips.

"I hope he rests in peace." Jared squeezes the bridge of his nose. "I'm tired. Why don't we get some sleep?" Jared turns his back on me and takes out another T-shirt. "Let it go, Layla."

I close my mouth and swallow my confusion. He seems more put together and not as scattered as he displayed only moments ago.

I'm not letting it go, but for now, I'll let it rest. I pull on the T-shirt and Jared lifts me before settling my head on the pillows. Without words, he drags the blanket over us and pulls me into his chest.

This close to him, he can't conceal what he doesn't want me to see. He's upset. The news has him shaken, and maybe he needs time to process it. I press a kiss to his chin before placing another on his lips.

"Good night." I have no idea how I'm going to sleep in Jared's arms. Everything about him was designed to wake me up.

"Good night." He holds me tighter, and for a while, we both pretend to be asleep until we finally aren't pretending anymore.

***

I'm tempted to run my finger along the bridge of his nose and then hold his nose, cutting off the air. I used to do this when we were kids, and he would wake up gasping for breath. It was hilarious. I'm half laughing as I reach out. His hand rises, and long fingers circle my wrist.

"Don't even think about it." He speaks with his eyes closed.

"How did you know?" I pull my hand back.

Jared opens one eye. "You're breathing and laughing all over me." Both eyes are open now, and I can sense him pulling away, retreating from me, and I don't understand.

My hand flutters to his chest. "I'm going to take a bath." I don't know how to seduce anyone, so I try again. "Your bathtub is huge."

He grins, and I see a small sparkle of interest. "Do you want me to run a bath for you?"

I'm not sure if my intentions are getting across. "No, I can do that." I roll out of the bed.

"Or I could get Kerry to do it for you," Jared offers.

I wave him off as I walk to the bathroom. "It's okay."

His bathroom is twice the size of mine, and the black-and-white theme carries on from his bedroom into here. The bathtub sits in the center of the room. The clawed-foot tub isn't a regular size; this one is so much bigger. I start to fill it and add some bubbles before opening up some cabinets in my search for towels. I find a stack and set them on the vanity table. I've only a T-shirt to strip off, so I keep it on as I step into the tub and sit on the edge. I watch the bubbles multiply as the water rises.

When the water reaches past my calf, I pull off the T-shirt but don't sink into the tub.

"I want to draw you." Jared's voice is rough.

I glance at him over my shoulder. My heart thumps in my chest, and I do the only thing I can think of, which is to sink into the tub. I move over to the taps and turn off the water. "Maybe you can later."

Jared steps into the bathroom, and I swallow with excitement as he pulls down his trousers. He never put on boxers, so his cock is on full display and he's aroused. Jared stops at the vanity and takes out a condom. He opens it while looking at me. Once he has the condom out, he rolls it onto his cock before giving it too long, slow strokes. My hand floats along the top of the water, moving bubbles aside.

Jared pulls off his shirt and discards it before stepping up to the tub. "You aren't very subtle."

My cheeks heat, but I don't shy away. "I'm only learning. I've never tried to seduce a man before." Jared gets into the bath, and having him naked beside me sends my heart racing. "Good. I'd hate to have to kill anyone." His remark is laced with a serious note I try to ignore.

I tilt my head and narrow my eyes. "Don't say things like that."

Jared sinks into the water and reaches for me. "I mean it. If anyone ever touched you"—he twirls a lock of my hair around his finger—"I'd kill them."

Jared pulls on my hair, dragging my face closer to his mouth. "This time, I get to fuck you."

Jared's hand cups the back of my head as he pushes me back into the water. Fear has me gripping the sides. My head thuds against the bathtub, and my grip loosens on the edge. His hands feel rough as they leave my hair and part my legs. Jared moves quickly and fills the space between them. The water sloshes across the tub and onto the floor at his quick movement.

I'm not ready for his entry, so when he pushes himself inside me in one controlled motion, I gasp, but I don't have a second to recover before he pulls out and slides inside me again. Water sloshes onto the floor at each jerk. Jared's head is buried in my neck. His arms grip the side of the tub, his muscles coiling and straining as he uses pulls his body into mine repeatedly. The burn and soreness steals my breath, but soon there's a nugget of pleasure that grows with each stroke.

The strength and awe of what's building inside me has me reaching out and gripping his forearms. I don't know if I want him to stop or continue. A part of me doesn't think I have a choice as he continues moving over my body, each jerk faster and harder than the one before. Air nips my legs as the water continues to slosh out. I'm aware of everything, down to Jared's hair that brushes my cheek, and his breathing that whooshes in my ear. Blood pounds in my ears, and each time Jared pumps into me, my head thuds on the bathtub while taking me to a new height. My body starts to quiver as Jared groans in my ear. His movements grow quicker, and there's a violence in his motion that has me sinking my nails into his forearms.

It's too much.

It's not enough.

His pumps become brutal against my body and my pleasure ebbs.

"You are mine. All of you," he declares and my arousal jumps. My hands leave his arm, and I give into him fully, spreading my legs as far as possible. I take the pain with the pleasure, but his words are the ribbon that ties the gift. I'm throbbing and squirming, and Jared has lost any semblance of control as he sinks fully into me. My heart has leapt into my throat at the unexpected orgasm that steals the air from my lungs before slamming into me with a force that has me trying to throw my head back.

Jared's movements are frantic before they cease with the cry of his own release.

CHAPTER EIGHTEEN

JARED

Anger leeches on to me, and no matter what I do, I can't seem to shake it off. Layla holds my hand, looking perfect in my letterman jacket. My mind keeps skipping to Nelson. It shouldn't. I shouldn't give two fucks what happened to him. His death had nothing to do with me. Yet, the voice that whispers in the back of my mind tells me his death had everything to do with me, because I know why he took his life.

"You okay?" Layla's wide, innocent eyes stare up at me. I reach out and touch her cheek. I don't ever want that innocence to leave her. She's pure and I'm tainted.

"Yeah," I answer while glancing over her shoulder at Alex, Abby, and Caroline, who walk toward us, linked arm in arm.

Perfect. I know exactly where to direct all my fucking anger.

Mark and Warren get out of their cars and walk toward us too. Layla tenses, and her shoulders curl forward like she's trying to make herself smaller. I want to hide her from them. I don't want them to have as much as one more second to hurt her in any shape or form.

"I love your jacket." Caroline steps up close to Layla, and I step between them, blocking her from Caroline. Caroline skips back away from me.

"You like older men," I say to Alex, wearing a grin.

Her lips drag down as she shrugs her shoulders and gives a short laugh. "Is that like a question?"

I want to grip her neck, but I laugh too. Layla tries to wriggle her fingers out of my hand, but I don't allow it. "No. It's not a question, Alex." My voice deadpans.

"Why so serious, Jay?" Caroline asks while unlinking herself from Alex.

"I don't know, Caroline." I allow my lips to turn up. "Maybe because Alex has been blowing my father."

Abby chokes before she goes into a coughing fit. Finally, Alex is affected. Her cheeks deepen in color. Warren sneers behind me, and Layla attempts to pull her hand out of mine again, but I don't allow it. I tighten my hold. I'm sure Layla wants to run off right about now. This would be uncomfortable for her, but I want her to witness me tear Alex down.

"I mean, I know your blow jobs are good, but my old man? Really?" I sneer.

"Stop it," Alex grits through her teeth. Her gaze fills with tears. Tears that I intend to spill in front of everyone. Other students are filing into the school, and it's a perfect opportunity. I release Layla's hand and turn, climbing to stand on the hood of my car.

"What are you doing?" Alex's panic is perfection.

"Have you heard, folks?" I shout and some students stop, while others make their way toward us. "Alex and my father are at it like rabbits." Laughter and gasps shoot out from the crowd.

Alex's face is taut with pure fear. I don't look at Layla; I keep my focus on Alex. "I even have the footage to back it up. You want to say anything to that, Alex?" I'm keeping my voice loud.

"Please stop!" she begs.

I jump down off the hood of the car and land beside her. "I haven't even fucking started."

"Jared." Layla's voice is to my left, and I know if I look at her, I'll break. I remind myself this is for her.

"You are pathetic," I say to Alex.

Tears stream down her face.

"Lying about your parents' divorce? Pathetic. Lies, that's all you ever tell." I lean in closer as she cries. "You were right when you said no one likes you."

"Jared." Layla's voice is stronger, but it doesn't matter. The damage is done as Alex barrels past me and through the crowd, screaming for everyone to get out of her way. Abby and Caroline don't follow her, and I feel nothing but disgust for them.

I finally look at Layla. Her chest rises and falls rapidly, and her cheeks have lost all color. Her mouth opens and closes while I reach out to take her hand. She doesn't pull away. I salute Warren, and Mark has his back to me before he chases after Alex. The crowd parts for me and Layla as I walk us up to the school.

"She won't bother you again."

Layla pulls her hand out of mine. "Jared. That was cruel."

I can't stop the smile that springs to my face. "That's not cruel Layla. That's justice. She got what was coming to her. "

Layla's brows drag down. "It didn't have to be by you."

"No, that's where you're wrong. It had to be by me. That's the only way she'll learn."

Layla gives a bitter laugh. "I forgot you're king of the school."

I step closer to Layla and tilt my head. "Don't get like that with me. I did it for you."

Layla folds her arms across her chest. "You shouldn't have." Her focus leaves me, and I follow her line of sight to Ashley. The moment Ashley's gaze clashes with mine, she runs off.

Smart.

"She won't talk to me," Layla whispers, and while she's half-distracted, I clear the distance between us and capture her face in my hands.

"I love you. That's all that matters." I press a kiss to her mouth, which is still dragged down. When we break the kiss, her frown isn't as severe.

"I love you, too."

I kiss her again, and when she smiles, I start to walk while holding her hand. "Of course you do. I am, after all, king of the school," I tease.

Layla isn't ready to joke. I walk her to class, and I don't leave until her lecture starts. I depart to find Warren. He's outside, making out with a girl. I don't have to ask how he passes his classes. The same way I do: money.

Money talks. Or in our case, gets us good grades and out of class.

Warren breaks the kiss and takes a piece of gum out of his mouth. "I think this is yours, love," he says, holding it out to the girl. She giggles and takes the gum, putting it back in her mouth. Warren notices me. "I might let you go down on me later." He winks at her before walking to me.

"Real Casanova," I say when he falls into step beside me.

"I'd say you're a heartbreaker, but I think you fucking smashed Alex's into oblivion. Remind me not to piss you off." Warren takes out his cigarettes and lighter.

"She had it coming." I defend my actions.

Warren lights up the cigarette. "Was she really fucking your dad?"

"Yeah." I stuff my hands in my jeans pockets.

"Is she good at giving blow jobs?" Warren asks.

I grin as I imagine Alex being propositioned by Warren. She'd run. He wouldn't be good enough for her. "Not bad," I answer.

"Might try her some time," Warren says.

I don't tell him that's not likely, but I honestly don't care if Alex blows the whole school.

"So Chester got arrested, and the paintings were recovered," he says.

I step out onto the lawn. "How did you get him to come home?" That's the part I can't piece together. Why did Chester make such a quick reappearance when my PI couldn't find him?

"You don't want to know." Warren raises a brow while he grins.

I face him. "I do." I'm fucking serious.

"Okay." Warren takes a drag of his cigarette. "We used bait to draw him out." Warren flicks the cigarette across the lawn.

Bait? I want to ask, but the wheels in my head start to turn. What could they have used?

"His son." Warren fills in the blanks.

My gut twists. Not the fucking kid. "I paid you to find Chester, not bring his kid into this."

Warren's demeanor changes, and he steps up to me. It's a clear reminder of who he is, but I don't back down from him. "I got the job done. A thank you would be nice. And the kid is fine."

I scratch my neck. "Thanks."

Warren flashes a quick grin. "So, does that mean I can cancel the other job?"

It takes me a minute to think about the other job. "No. I still want him dead. Now we have a time and place. After his court case, have someone there to take him out. I'm pushing for it next week, so it should be a quick trial."

Warren grins. "Is that why you flushed him out? So you could clip him at the courthouse? I like the way you think, Jay. Ever think of becoming a criminal, call me."

I laugh. "I'm flattered."

"We don't let people into our circle, so you should be."

I'm ready to answer Warren when I spot my mother standing at my car. "Fuck's sake. I'll catch you later." I fist-bump Warren before walking over to her to see what she wants.

"Do I need to call security?" I practically shout at her.

She spins around, and my body seems to bend toward her like it recognizes her as my mother.

"Jared. I just want a moment."

I stop at the hood of my car and lean against it. Folding my arms across my chest, I raise a brow. "Your time has already started." I shouldn't be entertaining her, but I still have some pent-up anger I need to get rid of. "Start speaking, Maura."

She doesn't like that I used her name. "I couldn't come by the house again, as he changed the code on the gate."

"I'm sorry. Do you want the new code? I can't understand why he would lock you out." Sarcasm drips from every word.

My mother steps closer. "It's not safe here," she whispers.

I lean in. "Then leave," I whisper back.

"Jared, all he wants is your money." My mother holds my stare.

I nod and unfold my arms. "It's always about money, isn't it?"

Color leaks out of her cheeks. "Sadly, yes."

"What if I don't want the money? Have you ever thought of that?" I push off my car and tower over my mother. "Stay away from me." I give my warning and turn to get into my car.

"The problem isn't if you want the money or not, Jared. The problem is *he* wants it, and at any cost." Her voice rises with emotion.

I unlock my car, and I'm ready to climb in. I'm hesitant with my next words, but they beg to be voiced. "I had a dream that I was about six and Dad was on the bathroom floor. He'd cut his wrists, and I was standing in his blood."

I pause and wait for her to say something, but she doesn't. I turn to face her, and tears stream down her face.

"I tried to hide you after that. I was terrified for you."

I grit my teeth and tighten my jaw. "See, this is the fucking thing. Nothing you say makes sense. And I know you're full of shit."

She sniffles and wipes falling tears from her eyes. "I'm trying to warn you."

"Leave me alone."

I get into the car and start the engine, but my mother stands at the window.

"Just promise me you won't sign anything."

I'm staring into her watery eyes. I don't answer her as I push my foot to the floor and drive home. I need to see my father's wrists. I need to see if all of this is in my head or if it happened. I don't recall him having scars, but I need to put my mind at rest, once and for all.

CHAPTER NINETEEN

LAYLA

One of Jared's security drops me back to his home, as Jared was 'caught up.' I wasn't too sure what that meant. Kerry, Andrea, and Amanda are waiting for me when I arrive home from school. I politely dismiss them with the promise I'll eat the food that was laid out for me.

I walk to the window where the table and small chairs are nestled. It's an odd feeling not having Jared at my side. I'm so used to his company that I find myself calling him.

Music floats in the background when he answers. He turns the volume down, but not before I catch a note. "What are you listening to?" I ask.

"Florence and the Machine."

My lips tug up. "I wouldn't have pictured you as a Florence fan." I pick up one half of the sandwich and look to see what it is. A chicken salad sandwich.

"What kind of music would you have pictured, then?"

"Maybe like techno or something," I say, placing the food back down on the plate.

My answer elects a soft laugh from Jared. "Nah. Not my thing. So, I hope you are eating?"

I sit down and open the can of soda. It crackles close to the phone. "Satisfied?"

"That's not food, Layla."

I chew my lip. "I'm just about to put on a horror show if you want to join me." I want to ask why he didn't come home with me, but I also need to give him some space.

"Yeah? Since when do you watch horrors? Remember that one time Nelson put on the advertisement for Freddy Kruger and you lost it?" Jared sounds like he's smiling.

I try to overlook my heightened heart rate at Nelson's name, but I'm also glad that Jared is speaking about him.

"That wasn't funny, Jared. I had nightmares for years."

"We're going to watch it one day. You have to conquer your fears."

I snort at the stupidity. "Sure. Keep thinking that."

"We are. It's a promise."

I groan, sitting back in the chair, but a part of me is excited about the future promise. Not the movie, but knowing we get to spend more time with each other. That this won't end between us.

I can hear Jared's gritty laugh, and an image of his smiling face and dimples fills my mind. I pick up the sandwich and take a bite. "So..."

Silence drags out. "So..." Jared says, and I get the feeling he knows I'm curious about where he is. "I'm on my way home. My father sent me to pick up some paperwork for him," he finally says. "Like he doesn't have a million flunkies to do it for him."

"You don't need to explain yourself."

"I know, but I wanted to. I'll be home soon."

I nod but remember he can't see me. "Okay."

I hang up, and the overwhelming level of relief at the thought of Jared coming home hits me hard and fast. I take another bite of the sandwich mechanically and sip my soda as I wait for him to arrive home.

A knock at the door has me rising from the chair, but I don't get far as the door opens. My hands immediately go to my back as Jared's father steps in.

"Am I okay to enter?" he asks.

I want to point out that he already has, but I force a smile. "Of course, Mr—"

He holds up his index finger in warning.

"Athar," I finish.

He smiles. "Are you settling in okay?"

He glances around my room, and I find myself doing the same. "I have more than I could possibly ever need."

He nods his head. "I'm sure it's a huge difference for you. But it's a lifestyle that most of us can get used to."

An uncomfortable silence falls around the room, and somewhere in the deepest part of my mind, I know he isn't here to be friendly. The thought startles me, and I find my shoulders growing stiffer.

"Jared has been so kind." The words fall flat. I'm at a loss for what to say.

"Jared is reckless with money, but"—his fingers flutter in front of him—"that's not why I'm here."

Once again, I'm at a loss for words, but this time I don't reach for filler conversation.

Athar closes the door behind him. "Jared's mother has tried to contact him on more than one occasion."

"I didn't know." I don't like the idea of being trapped in a room with Athar. My own thoughts shock me.

"I know you didn't. Jared is private." Athar smiles kindly at me, but the smile carries an undercurrent that scrapes against my flesh.

"Is there something I can do?" I ask.

Athar exhales loudly. "Actually, there is. But you won't like it, Layla Masters."

I don't like him using my full name. I'm glancing at the door, hoping Jared arrives at any second. Athar follows my line of sight. "He's not coming. I sent him on an errand so we could have some time to talk."

The room grows tighter by the second.

"I think this will be easier if I show you." Athar walks to the door and opens it. "It won't take long."

He leaves and I stand for a moment, wondering what to do. Then my feet start to clear the space, and I'm following Jared's father out into the hall and up the stairs.

"Jared is a sweet kid with a very loving streak. But at times, that love turns obsessive." Athar glances at me. "It becomes unhealthy, and that triggers a darkness in him."

"A darkness?" I ask as we step up onto the landing where I was shot.

"Yes, Layla. A darkness." He stops walking and faces me. "Do you know what my son asked me when he came home today?"

I shake my head.

"He wanted to see my wrists. He was looking for scars because he believes I tried to kill myself when he was a kid."

Now I'm looking for scars on Athar's wrists.

Athar laughs, but it's not humorous as he lifts the sleeves of his jacket.

Embarrassment at being caught scorches my cheeks.

"No marks."

He's right, there are none, but I'm getting more and more confused by the second. "I'm sorry, Athar, but what does this have to do with me?"

He nods. "Let me show you." We continue walking as Athar fixes the sleeves of his jacket. He pauses outside the door that's always locked, the one I wondered what it held. Jared said it was storage.

"The key my son wears around his neck is for this room."

My heart roars, and when he opens the door, a part of me wants to turn and run. I'm not prepared for what I step into.

Athar flicks on the light, and I gasp as the blood roars and crashes against my eardrums.

My mind is taking in all the drawings, but I don't think I'm processing it. I'm cold as I step into the chaotic room.

"Jared is obsessed with you. I understand what you both went through as kids, but when he first came here, we couldn't stop this." His father moves his hand around the room.

There isn't an inch that isn't covered with my face. It's all too much. My legs buckle, and I reach out to steady myself.

Athar takes my arm. "I'm sorry, Layla. I didn't want to show you this. But I also need you to understand that Jared isn't well. A few years ago, Jared finally locked this room, and we witnessed him getting better." Athar stops talking.

My vision blurs. "Until I resurfaced," I finish.

He nods. "It's not just the drawings. He thinks I'm trying to get his money. He even accused me of sleeping with Alex, a friend of his."

Oh, God. It wasn't true about Alex? He humiliated her at school.

"I fear my son is in far more trouble than I thought."

I face Athar. "What do you mean?"

"I don't want to worry you."

My fingers sink into Athar's arm. "Please. If I can help..."

"He's been seen with Warren O'Reagan."

I nod. "That's his friend."

"Warren O'Reagan is in the Mafia, and my son has been transferring money to him. I don't know why. I was hoping you would."

This keeps getting worse by the second. "I don't know," I admit. I need to sit.

"If we don't find out what he's up to, he may end up in trouble." Athar's voice is filled with doom.

I release his arm.

"Ask him," I say. "Jared won't lie."

Athar looks at me like I'm stupid. "He might tell you, but he won't tell me. Right now, he thinks I'm the enemy." Athar glances around the room. "We need to keep this between us."

I can't deceive Jared. "I don't think I can do that."

"If you love him, you will." Athar holds out his arm. "We'd better go before he returns."

I leave the room in a daze.

I don't have a moment to recover before Athar starts to hurry. He's on his phone, and then in a flash, he puts it away. "He's home. I hope you can help me, Layla. I want to make sure my son is safe, and you are the person he trusts the most these days."

I nod as my heart pounds. Athar squeezes my shoulder before leaving me alone.

I'm on the second floor when Jared appears. Fear curls in my stomach. I try to shake it off, but I wonder how well I know him.

He pauses, and his smile falls from his face. "What's wrong?" He's looking past me.

"I was just remembering." The lie has me wrapping my arms around my waist.

Jared zones in on me.

"The shooting," I finish and continue down the stairs. My heart beats rapidly as I approach Jared.

He moves to the center of the steps, blocking me. "Are you sure that's all?"

"Is it not enough?" I ask and sniffle. I need space. I need to think.

"Jesus. Of course, Layla." He grips my forearms and gently rubs them. "You shouldn't be up here."

I drop my gaze to the floor. "I just think I need to lie down." I manage to wriggle out of his grasp. He's heavy on my heels, and I try not to run, but I don't know why I'm feeling panicked.

"Don't you want to watch the movie?" Jared asks from behind me.

I reach the ground floor. "Maybe later." I'm expecting him to leave me, but he follows me to my room. Kerry is at the door.

"Could you get me some Tylenol? I have a headache," I explain. Kerry departs to get me the tablets.

"What made you go up there?" Jared asks.

"I was bored." I shrug, but I can't make eye contact when I finally look up at him as he's watching me. God, I hate lying to him, but all I have to think about is that room. I swallow. "I won't be going back up there," I say.

"Chester will be behind bars soon, Layla. Right now, he's in custody. You have nothing to fear." Jared steps closer to me, and I try not to flinch. I know he would never hurt me.

"What about the gun? What if Chester tells them?" I ask. Why isn't that important anymore?

"I don't think anyone will believe him."

"You did before," I point out.

Jared takes another step closer. "Yes, but that was before he was caught with all our stolen paintings."

Did he even steal them?

My head hurts too much.

Kerry arrives back and pauses in the door. I hold out my hand for the tablets and water as she enters. "I'm going to lie down," I tell Kerry.

"Shall I draw the curtains?" she asks.

"Please, Kerry," I say as I drink down the painkillers. When I empty the glass, I look at Jared.

"I'll let you get some rest. If you need me, I'll just be next door." That didn't sound comforting. I nod and wait until he and Kerry are gone before locking the door. My vision wavers, and I cover my mouth with my hands as I start to cry.

CHAPTER TWENTY

LAYLA

THE MORNING COMES TOO soon. I'm tired, and my eyes feel grainy. I scrub my face, hoping to bring some life back into it. I look so much paler than I usually do. Getting dressed for class, I ignore the knock on my door and the soft words from Kerry. I tie my hair up in a high ponytail and try to center myself. Today at school, I'm going to ask Warren about Jared.

Every time I think of everything that Athar told me last night, my head spins. So, one thing at a time. I don't want Jared to get into trouble, so finding out what he and Warren are up to is what I'm going to focus on today.

The knock at my bedroom door again has me taking one final look around my room before I open it.

"Good morning," Kerry says. "Your breakfast is ready in the dining room with Master Jay and his father."

Breakfast with Jared and his father. My chest tightens as I leave the room and make my way to the dining room. My heart betrays me as I look at Jared. His dimples appear, and he stands when I enter.

"How are you feeling?" His concern has guilt haunting me.

"Better." I steady my breathing as I walk to the table.

Athar lowers his newspaper. "Good morning, Layla."

"Good morning, Athar."

Jared pulls out a chair for me beside him. A stack of pancakes and a steaming cup of tea are waiting for me. "Thank you." My heart pounds in my chest, and I don't reach for the knife and fork. Instead, I place my hands on my lap to make sure they're steady.

"Jared was telling me you had a bad headache. Pesky things, they are." Athar eats a spoonful of his cereal.

"I'm all better now," I say as I decide my hands are steady enough to pick up my knife and fork. I eat while Jared's presence beside me has my nerves jangled. He's watching me, and each time our gazes clash, I want to cave in and just ask him what's going on. I want to ask about the secret room. I want to ask why he's hiding so much from me. I look away before he can see the hurt in my eyes.

I keep my mouth full so I don't have to talk. Athar returns to reading his morning paper.

"We'd better get going," Jared says.

I'm so happy to be released from the table. I take a large gulp of tea, and when I look at Jared, he's grinning.

"That headache sure worked up an appetite."

I place my knife and fork on my plate and thank Athar for breakfast before following Jared to the garage. When we're about to get in the car, Jared stops, and with the keys in his hands, he tilts his head.

"You okay?" His brow draws down, and he rattles the keys.

"Yeah, I'm fine." I widen my eyes before forcing a smile and getting into the car.

Once again, I'm struggling to remain calm and silent with the knowledge I have. I don't think I'll make it to the end of the day. I keep stealing glances at Jared, and all I want to do is crack and confess to what I know.

But I stay strong, and when we reach the school, there's no time for chatting, as my class is about to start. Jared walks me to class, and he looks troubled. I hate that I've put that look on his face, but once I find out what he and Warren are up to, maybe I can help in some way.

Yeah, maybe.

***

Lunchtime arrives, and Jared is waiting for me outside my third class. It's warm, so everyone has opted to eat outside. Jared hands me a sandwich and a plastic disposable cup that's filled with tea. A girl I recognize from the beach party gives me a quick smile.

"Hi. I think I know you." She points at me.

"Yeah, I know you from Mark's beach party," I say. I notice that both Mark and Alex aren't sitting with us on the lawn. But Warren is. He's right beside the girl from the beach party. He's lying back on his elbows staring up at the sky. Jared's leg brushes against mine.

The girl smiles widely, and silver sparkles in her mouth from her tongue ring. "Sally." She gives a quick wave. "I vaguely remember you. I think I was drinking more than I was serving."

I smile at her. "Yeah, well, I didn't fare too well either, so..."

Sally smiles before looking back at Warren. She nudges his leg. Warren stops staring at the sky and focuses on Sally.

"What?" he asks.

"You're quiet." She's still smiling. Her tongue flicks out, and she licks her lips.

"Are you bored? I can give you something to keep you occupied." Warren sits forward, and Sally leans further into him.

"Maybe later." She kisses him before getting up and waving at me. "Nice meeting you again."

"You too, Sally," I say, realizing I never told her my name. She leaves, and I don't turn to Abby and Caroline, who sit a few feet away from us.

"Could you get me a soda?" I ask Jared sweetly. He doesn't question me, and I feel so bad when he presses a kiss to the crown of my head before getting up.

"Sure, no problem."

I nibble on the sandwich and look to make sure Jared is out of earshot. I know I don't have much time.

"You and Jared are close," I start, leaning toward Warren.

Warren sits up and both brows rise while a ghost of a smile plays on his lips.

"I know something is going on between the two of you," I continue as my heart races.

"If you're worried I'm going to steal him"—he raises both hands—"I can assure you, he's all yours." His grin holds humor.

My heart pounds heavier in my chest, and I glance toward the college before speaking to Warren.

"Is he in some sort of trouble?" I ask. "I love him, and I can't bear to think about anything happening to him."

Warren's smile leaves his face, and he moves closer. I'm holding my breath. He's going to tell me what's going on.

"Do you know who I am?" he starts.

"I don't care who you are. All I know is that something is going on, and I want to know what."

More amusement flashes across Warren's face. He looks over my shoulder. "I think you're asking the wrong person." He lies back, placing his hands under his head.

I'm confused until a can of soda appears in front of me. My gaze is drawn to the black ink band around Jared's wrists. How much did he hear?

I reach up and take the can. "Thank you," I whisper and keep my fingers tight around it. I don't open the can as Jared sits back down. Once I gather some courage, I finally look at him.

His gaze looks troubled, and when he glances at Warren, anger tightens his features.

"I was asking Warren about Sally," I lie.

Jared picks at the grass—well, tearing it is more accurate.

"She just seems so nice," I continue and I know I need to shut up.

Warren remains lying back, sunbathing, doing nothing to help me.

Jared's eyes appear almost black. "Aren't you going to drink your soda?" he asks.

I feel like I've been caught conspiring against him. My heart hurts, and I reach out and touch his hand. "Thank you for getting me this," I say.

His features soften slightly.

Ashley freezes when our gazes meet, and she's ready to run off. We haven't talked in a long time, and right now, I want to avoid all of Jared's questions, so I quickly get up.

"I'll be back in a minute." I walk quickly.

"Ashley," I call.

She doesn't stop, but I know she hears me. "Ashley." I catch up to her, and she finally stops walking. "You've been avoiding me."

"I've just had a lot on my mind," she says, but she doesn't have that normal Ashley attitude I've become accustomed to.

"Me too," I admit. How I wish I could talk to someone about all this.

"You look tired," Ashley says, and she reaches out and briefly touches my arm.

"Yeah, rough day yesterday."

Ashley raises a sharp eyebrow, encouraging me to continue. The action makes me smile. It's so like her.

"Honestly, I don't want to talk about it. So tell me all about Nicco. He's worth talking about."

Ashley smiles like the proud mother she is, and it's so nice just to chat with her. "Before we start talking about my adorable son"—her huge smile is contagious, and my lips rise—"I want to talk about the night you babysat."

Both our smiles fade. I nod, letting her continue.

Ashley looks nervous as she chews her lip. "So, you know Chester's Nicco's father."

I want to ask if that happened in a drunken moment, but I remain silent and find myself reaching up and touching my shoulder.

Guilt fills Ashley's gaze, and now I wonder if that's why she's been avoiding me.

"Chester and I have been off and on since we were kids. But it's over for good now, so his coming over the other night wasn't something I thought would happen. And finding out what he did to you..." She rubs the back of her neck, pain radiating from her gaze. "I didn't think he would be capable of such violence."

"It's fine, Ashley. Honestly. Chester is going to be locked away, and I think that's good for everyone."

Ashley frowns.

"Seriously, we are good. And it won't put me off babysitting Nicco," I say, and Ashley smiles at me.

I take a peek at where Jared was sitting with Warren, but he's no longer there. Neither is Warren. *Shit. I should have kept an eye on them.* Someone I don't want to see is making their way toward us.

"What's wrong?" Ashley asks, turning around before facing me again. "Oh, God. I heard what happened with her and Jared."

Alex's long hair is done in braids that fall down her back. She looks fabulous today, just as she always does, though I hate admitting that.

Her dark leather pants look like they're painted on, but she has the figure to wear them, and she paired them with a small green tank top, which showcases her ample bust. When she reaches us, she looks at me. "I was wondering if I could have a word."

Ashley tuts while rolling her eyes, and I sink my heels into the ground. "Don't start, Alex," Ashley tells her. "Seriously, Layla doesn't want to hear it."

Oh, that's harsh, and there is a moment of vulnerability on Alex's face, but she covers it up. A sharpness enters her features.

Alex doesn't respond to Ashley. "Fine, I'll say my piece here. I've been friends with Jay for years, and we've never had a bad word between us." Alex shakes out her shoulders. "Until you arrived. But I get it, and I'm willing to forgive you."

Forgive me? I want to ask for what. I don't need any grief from Alex. I'm scanning the area again for Jared and Warren, but they're nowhere in sight.

"I'm trying to fix things here, Layla. You could at least answer me."

"I don't know what you want, Alex." I finally focus on her. "I think you need to talk to Jared. Not me."

Alex doesn't like my answer, her lips pulling into a thin line, but she brushes her hair back off her shoulder. "I'll let him know we've patched things up."

I'm too distracted to really care. "Okay," I reply.

"Can we chat later?" I reach out and touch Ashley's arm.

She frowns but nods. "Yeah, of course."

I don't wait around but head to the parking lot. I call Jared's phone, but it goes to voicemail.

Shit.

CHAPTER TWENTY-ONE

LAYLA

THE REST OF THE day drags, and when classes end, Jared is nowhere in sight. William is waiting for me in the parking lot. Jared's car is gone.

Without a word, I climb into the back, and William closes the door behind me. On the way home, I call Evelyn after seeing a few missed calls from her.

"I've been trying to call you all day," she says, but her voice is light, telling me it isn't urgent.

"I left my phone on silent in my locker."

"Carl and I have been invited to a dinner for a charity. I just wanted to make sure you weren't coming home. I didn't want you to arrive and us not to be there."

I buckle my belt. "No, I've got loads of homework. Go enjoy yourself. You guys deserve it."

Evelyn's laughter is warm, trickling through the phone and settling on my shoulders. "I'm looking forward to it. So how is college?" Evelyn asks, and we chat easily as William drives me back to Jared's. The call ends on a nice note, and I'm smiling into the phone long after Evelyn hangs up.

The car stops, and it's my cue to remove my seat belt. I thank William as I enter the house. I stop by Jared's room, but he isn't there. I consider checking his drawers, but I won't invade his privacy like that.

No, instead you quiz his friends. The voice in my head mocks me as I make my way to my room.

I change into yoga pants and a gray T-shirt before letting my hair down. I massage my temples as I walk barefoot around the room. I've gone the wrong way about everything. Maybe I should have just asked Jared. I try to focus on my studies but find I'm checking my phone every ten minutes. The handle of my door rattles, and I climb off the bed as the door opens.

I take in a sharp breath.

"What happened?" The cut over Jared's eye looks pretty bad, and he has a bruised cheek to go with it. My heart thumps in my chest with worry.

Jared's lip twitches, and his cut eyebrow rises, only to drop back quickly. The pain is apparent.

I fold my arms across my chest as he closes the door behind him. He throws me a sidelong look and passes me before sitting down on my bed. I pivot so I'm facing him.

"Well, are you going to answer me?" I ask once a few more seconds have passed.

Jared starts to get up.

"Jared, sit down," I demand. His surprise at my tone lights up his eyes, but he does as I say. I'm a little surprised by my tone too, so I add, "Please" before getting a damp cloth from my bathroom. I return, bringing over one of the chairs and pulling it close to Jared. He accommodates me by spreading out his long legs on either side of my chair. I wasn't thinking about how intimate this position would be until now.

I dab the cut over his eye with the cloth. I have to pull my chair closer to him in order to reach. My heart picks up, and I flicker my gaze to Jared, who's observing me the whole time.

"This is going to sting," I tell him, and he nods, not speaking or taking his eyes off me. I can feel a slight tremor enter my hands. Guilt weighs heavily on my shoulders. Reaching out with my free hand, I hold his face. As I lean in, I can smell him, the uniqueness that is Jared. He closes his eyes just before I dab the cut. He doesn't flinch.

"Am I hurting you?" I ask, pausing. I just want to make sure.

"No." His one word sounds different, his tone deeper. He keeps his eyes closed as I wipe the cut.

"What happened?" I ask again, and he glances up at me. I bite my lip as I give a final dab, wishing he kept his eyes closed. The deep brown of his eyes makes me feel jittery. I lean away. The distance is minimal, but it's enough for me to get my bearings. Thankfully, the cut isn't deep.

"I got into a fight."

"Really? I would have never guessed." My sarcastic remark has his lips twitching. I don't find this funny. Jared reaches over and takes my free hand in his, entwining our fingers together. Looking down at our hands, I take in his damaged knuckles.

"Layla, I'm fine," Jared says, but my throat is tightening.

"Who did you fight with?" I ask. My suspicions are growing that it was Warren. I hope I'm wrong.

Jared's eyes darken, and he looks away. "Warren, and he deserved it," he finally says, looking back at me. I don't have to ask why. This is because I was talking to him.

"Stay still," I tell him while removing my hand from his. I need to get ointment for his cut. I leave him and find a first-aid kit in the bathroom. When I return, Jared hasn't moved. This time, he doesn't close his eyes. He watches me, and I nearly get ointment in his eye because he's making me so nervous. His breath brushes my neck, moving down the V of my T-shirt. Heat spreads up my neck and to my cheeks.

When I lean back, I focus on getting a Q-tip and antiseptic for his knuckles. My eyes dart to him as I get them ready. He's once again tracking every movement I make. When I sit back and take one of his large hands into my lap, he stretches out his fingers for me.

"It was a small fight."

I snort while dabbing the broken skin. He hisses, and I stop.

"Don't stop. It's fine," he says, so I continue. I don't want to hurt him, but if his cuts aren't cleaned, they could get infected.

"We're cool with each other," Jared continues.

I stop what I'm doing and narrow my eyes at him. "After you hit him?"

Jared's eyes darken once again. "Yes." He's serious, and I don't know what's worse: that he beat him up or that he still spoke to him after.

We're quiet as I finish his hands, and I realize that the bruise on his cheek isn't bad.

"Any more bruises or cuts?" I ask.

The corner of his mouth turns up. "Unfortunately not." His grin grows.

I don't smile. "What does that even mean?" *He wanted someone to hurt him?*

He quickly entwines our fingers together, making me look at him. "Layla, it was a joke." He dips his head, forcing me to look up at him.

"I'm not laughing, Jared."

"You're so gentle. I meant that I wish I had more wounds for you to clean."

The tips of my ears burn at the compliment. I don't feel I deserve it. "Oh. Okay then."

A small awkward laugh escapes my lips, and Jared's gaze flickers to them before returning to my eyes. He smiles with dimples and all.

My heart slows, along with my frantic thoughts. "You need to promise me no more fighting."

"It was only a bit of a scuffle. Seriously, stop worrying."

I raise a brow at him. *A scuffle?* I play with the Q-tip.

"So how bad does Warren look?" I ask as I wonder just how bad it is compared to Jared's face.

He gives me a guarded look. "Same as I do." The shrug he gives doesn't match his tone and look.

"You said no one ever gets a hit on you," I say and wish that it were still true. Seeing Jared injured hurts far worse than I ever expected it to.

"He's Warren O'Reagan. I had to let him get in a few hits."

"This isn't funny," I repeat and get up, only to have Jared grip my wrists.

His expression hardens. "What were you asking him?"

"About Sally," I lie and it falls flat.

He takes a deep breath, and I slowly lift my gaze until our eyes meet.

"Why are you lying to me?" Jared reaches out and touches my face. "You don't have to lie to me, Layla."

He's killing me. I swallow the lump in my throat and stare into his eyes. "I asked Warren what you two were up to." My pulse spikes as I speak.

His gaze is guarded.

"Are you in trouble?" I ask.

Jared stares at me as his hand leaves my face. "I'm only trying to help, Jared."

"You should have just asked me."

My chest burns with embarrassment. My mind is in a frenzy, trying to figure out how much I messed up.

His gaze bores into mine. "I would have told you." His serious tone has me nodding. I feel so far out of my depth right now. Our gazes are locked, and I think my chest is going to explode.

My lips part as I think of what I want to say.

A flash of uncertainty passes through his features.

"Then tell me, what dealings do you have with Warren O'Reagan?"

Jared reaches out and takes my hands before pulling me back into the chair I was previously sitting in. His legs clamp on either side of me, and I feel trapped. I think that's his intention.

He would never hurt me. I repeat the reminder in order to stay calm.

"First, tell me why you're asking." Jared shifts closer to the edge of the bed. If I leaned in slightly, our foreheads would touch. His hands trail along my arms until his fingers rest on my wrist. I glance down. His thumb strokes the tender flesh.

"Your heart is beating so fast, Layla."

I try to pull my hands back, and when Jared doesn't release them, I glare at him. "Let me go."

"Why? Are you afraid that I can tell when you're lying?"

I yank my hands again. "You think this is normal?"

He releases me before running his fingers through his hair.

"Your father said you made several large transactions to Warren O'Reagan and that you might be in a lot of trouble." My mouth keeps moving. "He said I'm the only person you trust."

Jared leans back, and the weight of my words pushes down on his wide shoulders. I hate the effect I'm having on him.

"You and my father were talking about me?" Hurt flashes in Jared's gaze.

"Yes. He showed me the room." I can't hold his stare. My gaze dances to the key that's hidden under his shirt. "He wanted me to help find out what you and Warren were up to."

"Anything else?" Jared growls.

"He said you're in contact with your mother and that you aren't..." I glance at Jared. The weight of a freight train slams into me. "Well," I finish.

I want to run and hide, but I keep my head high.

"Well?" Jared questions.

"He said you came home and checked his wrists for scars. He said that you believe he tried to take his life."

Jared exhales and rubs his mouth roughly. "So you had no headache last night? Just like you didn't have one the day you went dress shopping with Alex?"

I hate how disappointed he is. The urge to run again is choking, but I remain where I am.

"I think I avoid confrontation," I answer.

A ghost of a smile graces Jared's mouth. I don't know how he can smile right now. "I asked Warren what you two were talking about. He wouldn't tell me, but he said he liked you and thought you were very brave."

That sets me back.

"I told him you were the bravest person I know." Jared looks proud, then he tilts his head. "Then we got into a fight."

Jared reaches out but pauses before taking my hands. "You should have come to me, Layla."

"I'm sorry." I'm the one who takes Jared's hands in mine. I don't entwine our fingers, but I do something he did to me only moments ago. I run my middle and index finger along his wrist, feeling for his steady heartbeat.

His brow rises, and he grins. He doesn't stop me but holds still.

"Why did you send Warren money?" I ask.

"When Chester broke in and shot you, my father made it look like a burglary. He had William hide some of our artwork. Before we went to the Gardaí station, I hired Warren to put the artwork in Chester's house."

I hear the words, but I'm so focused on the steady beat of Jared's heart under my fingers that it's hard for them to register. "That's it? That's your dealings with him?"

"No." Jared leans closer. "You don't need to know all this, Layla."

"I beg to differ, Jared."

He nods. "I also needed him to flush Chester out so the Gardaí could capture him. I paid a PI, but he had no luck."

I want to smile. I want to rejoice that it's not that bad. Why did my mind go to drugs? I feared Jared getting involved with the Mafia.

"Is Warren actually Mafia?"

Jared grins. "Yes. He's the real deal."

I let that sink in. "Your father said you weren't well. What exactly did he mean?"

Jared's heart beats a bit faster under my fingers, yet he doesn't pull away.

"He thinks I'm obsessed with you." Jared pulls his wrists out of my fingers. "Maybe I am." He reaches up and cups my cheek. I lean into his touch. "The room was a place I could think of you, draw you. He didn't like it."

"I asked you about the key around your neck." I trail off. It doesn't really matter.

Jared surprises me when he pulls me onto his lap, my legs falling on either side of him. I wrap my arms around his neck. "I told you it was the key to my heart. I didn't lie."

My heart beats wildly.

"Any other questions?"

I focus on his lips and inhale the scent of him. I want to kiss him, but I also don't feel completely satisfied. He's giving me an answer for everything, but his gaze tells me there's so much more.

I lean my forehead against his. "Your mother. Tell me about her."

Jared tenses, and I know I've finally hit a sore spot.

"She put me in the foster system. What more can I say?"

I reach up and trace the outline of Jared's mouth. "I know this sounds horrible, but I'm glad she did. I'm glad I had you." I look at Jared. "I survived because of you, Jared, and I'm sorry for not being honest with you about your dad."

"He had no right going to you." Jared's tongue flicks out, and he licks my thumb.

"He was concerned." I start to defend Athar, but after speaking to Jared, I don't feel as unstable as his father made me feel.

"I'm not so sure," Jared says.

I lift my fingers from Jared's mouth and trace the outline of his brow. The one that isn't cut. "You might need stitches," I say.

He grins, raising the bruise on his cheek. "There is only one way to heal me."

I meet his gaze. "And what's that?"

"A kiss."

My lips touch his, and all the fear and anxiety that had built up seems to pour out of me, and I shuffle closer to Jared's solid body.

Jared's damaged hands roam across my ass, and when he pulls me heavily against him, his erection presses into my core. I push him back, and without a second's hesitation, Jared lies back and I straddle him. He makes me feel powerful with how he's looking at me. Awe and pleasure mix together in the depths of his eyes.

When I bend my head to press a kiss to his lips, his hands circle my wrists, and he drags them against his chest. "Don't ever lie to me again."

I swallow at the visible anger in his gaze.

I nod, but that acknowledgment doesn't seem like enough for Jared. "I won't."

He takes some pressure off my wrists before pulling me down on top of him. Our mouths smash together. His tongue enters my mouth, and I'm out of control as I give over to the need to have him.

I give a startled cry as his hands move under my shirt and wiggle their way under my bra. His fingers knead and squeeze my breasts, and I'm not ready for the flood of wetness that pools between my legs.

Jared moves quickly, and I find him on top of me while I stare up at him. His hands roam across my upper body. I do nothing but lie there and close my eyes. When his hands leave my skin, I open my eyes to find Jared removing his clothes. I'm kicking off my own shoes and socks as he walks naked and erect to the drawer. I've removed the rest of my clothes when he returns with a condom on.

My heart pounds as I think of the bath and how conflicting it felt. As Jared climbs back onto the bed, that conflicting feeling flees. He grips my legs and pulls my body hard against his. He's so much bigger than me, and his body smothers mine while he supports his upper body on his elbows. His flesh is warm against mine as his hands grip my thighs and direct my core to his cock. I hold my breath as I wait for the pain, but it doesn't come as Jared dips only the tip inside me. I close my eyes at the perfect feeling as he moves in slowly before pulling out.

"Look at me."

I do as Jared commands, and it's like an out-of-body experience as I stare into the dark abyss of his eyes. He moves with a perfect rhythm in and out of me, getting deeper when I'm stretched to take it. It's perfect, and I reach up to touch his bruised cheek.

"I love you."

Jared pauses before he turns his face and presses a kiss to the inside of my hand. "I love you too, Layla."

We stare into each other's eyes as Jared continues to move smoothly inside me. I can sense the build, but I don't want it to end.

I close my eyes but open them when Jared reminds me to keep looking at him.

His face tightens as he, too, closes in on what we both seek, and I stop holding back. My hands reach out and grip his shoulders as he speeds up inside me, and the thoughts of Jared coming inside me have me moving my hips along with him.

"Oh, fuck." He groans and I move my hips faster. He mimics my speed, and I know I can't hold on much longer.

Jared pumps harder. His features strain just as I reach a height before I come, and he joins me in ecstasy.

CHAPTER TWENTY-TWO

JARED

IT'S THE MORNING OF the court case. We only found out last night that it would be held today. My father's legal team had worked tirelessly to pull this off, and I'm impressed at the speed they did it in.

Layla stands in front of the mirror, fixing her black suit jacket. She's been doing the same thing for the last ten minutes. I loosen the collar of my shirt. I'll close the top two buttons before we leave the house.

"I wish you didn't have to do this, but my father has assured me the proceedings will be quick." I reach out and touch Layla's shoulder. She lays her hand on top of mine.

"I'm the only one who can identify him." Layla turns, and my hand falls away from her. "It will be quick, like ripping off a Band-Aid."

My father promised that Layla would be on the stand for only a few moments, and I have to believe him. I have no choice. But I'm still fuming with him for being a colossal asshole. Showing Layla the room and trying to turn her against me is something I'm not willing to forgive or forget.

Layla reaches up and touches my cut brow gently. "You're frowning." She forces her lips into a smile.

"I just want this over with." I'm antsy as I think of what will happen after the court case. Warren said the sniper would be in place. I'm assuming he'll be in one of the surrounding buildings. I consider calling it off, but as I stand here in front of

Layla, I know I'm making the right decision. Chester deserves to die. The callousness with which he shot Layla point-blank can't go unpunished.

"Me too," Layla confesses.

Layla is quiet as we gather the last of our belongings. Carl and Evelyn are going to meet us at the courthouse. My father wants to drive us, but I don't want to be in his presence, so I drive myself and Layla to Navan Courthouse. The courtyard we pull into doesn't have many cars. We're early. The traffic was light this morning, which I hadn't expected. Normally, it's busy with primary school commuters.

Evelyn and Carl are sitting in Carl's Mercedes across from us. Evelyn nods at me before she bends down and sits back up.

"You just have to identify him, and that's it." I grip Layla's hand. If I could do it for her, I would. I fucking hate that she has to take the stand.

Layla nods. "It will be over quickly."

"Like ripping off a Band-Aid." I repeat her earlier words and get a genuine smile out of her. Evelyn gets out of the car, and Carl follows behind. Layla lifts our joined hands and presses a kiss to mine before releasing it.

"I'm going to say hi to Evelyn and Carl." Layla speaks as she removes her seat belt and scoops her bag up off the floor.

"I'll be with you in a minute." I move the rearview mirror and button up my shirt, then I straighten my tie.

Layla gets out and closes the door. Carl waves at me, and I salute him before fixing the mirror and gathering my phone and keys. I'm tempted to text Warren to make sure everything is in place, but he hasn't let me down yet. Even after our fistfight, he said it changed nothing between us. He smiled and licked blood off his lip before declaring he hadn't enjoyed a fight like that in a while. I'm tempted to touch my brow, but I focus on getting out of the car, trusting that Warren will keep his word.

Walking around the hood, I lock the car before I join Layla, Evelyn, and Carl.

"That's a nasty cut you have," Evelyn says, eyeing my face. She wraps an arm around Layla's shoulder, pulling her closer. I'm beginning to think that Evelyn doesn't see how overprotective she is when it comes to Layla. But, I'm glad for it today. I think Layla needs a mother's touch.

"A friendly boxing match." I touch my cut brow like it doesn't sting like a bitch.

Evelyn raises both brows. "I wouldn't like to see if it was unfriendly."

Carl steps forward and holds out his hand. "Great seeing you again."

I take his hand and shake it. "You too, Carl." He's actually a decent man who is good to Layla.

My father arrives. He pulls his car next to mine and smiles at us all. I don't smile back, and Layla seems to stiffen. I wouldn't have been surprised if he arrived in his helicopter, but I'm also glad he didn't make a spectacle of himself.

"We should go in." Evelyn speaks to Layla.

"Go ahead. I'll be there in a minute," I say to Layla.

Layla is sandwiched between Carl and Evelyn as they walk to the courthouse. My father approaches, and I don't let him fall into step beside me.

"Where is your legal team?" I ask as he trails behind me.

"Inside." My father grips my arm, stopping me from walking. "We need to look united, son."

I step closer to my father. "Take your hand off me."

He does and uncertainty has his gaze darting around the space. I'm sure he's wondering who is watching.

"Stay out of my way," I warn as I turn and make my way into the courthouse. My father's legal team stands together with files pressed tightly against their chests. They laugh and chat. Their suits cost more than some of the cars in the parking lot. I approach them, and they fall silent.

"I want Layla's questioning kept short and to the point," I remind them. "If anyone drags it out…" I let my threat hang over their heads as I meet each of them with a hard gaze.

"They already know this, Jay." My father steps up beside me. "My men will do a great job."

"I don't care what happens. Just make sure Layla isn't on the stand long," I say again before pushing my hands into my trouser pockets. Having my hands trapped stops me from poking them in the chest to drive my words home.

"We will. We think we can get the maximum sentence of ten years."

My father looks proud as his solicitor speaks up. I don't care if Chester walks out of here a free man. As long as he leaves this courthouse to give the sniper his moment to take him out, that's all that matters to me. Nothing else.

Layla is inside the main courtroom. She's at the front, with Evelyn and Carl two seats behind. I join her. Opening my suit jacket, I sit down.

"How are you?" I ask.

Her complexion is stark white. I reach for her hand and squeeze her fingers before looking over my shoulder as my father's legal team makes their way to us.

"Water off a duck's back," Layla whispers under her breath.

A few more people are in the courtroom. I spot Ashley at the back. She's not looking around and is focused on a device in her hands. My father speaks to random people as he makes his way slowly to us. He thinks he's a local celebrity. A lull falls around the room as Chester arrives in chains. Two Gardaí escort him in. His solicitor isn't far behind.

I'm waiting for the judge to arrive so this can be quick. Judge Berwick has been paid handsomely to make this an open-and-shut case. He will rule in whatever way my father's legal team deems fit.

Judge Berwick arrives out onto his stage, and everyone rises. I release Layla's hand and look over at Chester. He's grinning at me, and rage has me facing forward before I do something fucking stupid like dashing across the room and plummeting my fist into his face. He thinks he'll get away with this.

It takes a lot of force to keep me facing forward. The case starts, and after the details are delivered from both sides, Layla is called to the stand. My father's legal team keeps to their word, and the questioning is over promptly. Layla points at Chester, declaring he is the one who shot her. She's released from the stand. She walks back to me, her gaze locked on the floor.

I don't care about all the rest of the jargon. The doctors, Inspector Reilly, and William all take the stand. Time ticks away painfully slow, and it still takes another twenty minutes before Chester's ruling is handed down. He gets the maximum sentence. Ten years.

He pulls against his handcuffs, the force rocking the two Gardaí on either side of him. It's my turn to grin as I take pleasure in Chester's outburst as he's dragged past me.

I take Layla's hand and wait a few minutes as Chester is pulled from the courtroom. "I'm so proud of you," I whisper into her ear.

"It's over." She smiles up at me. There's more relief on her face than anything else. Evelyn and Carl hug Layla.

"You did so well." Evelyn presses a kiss on Layla's forehead.

I'm trying to stay present with them, but I'm waiting for a gunshot. I'm waiting to hear the wails of panic. I'm waiting, but nothing happens. I wonder if the gun will have a silencer or if we'll hear the bang.

We continue leaving as more people arrive in the courtroom for the next case to be heard. The crowd is far larger than what we had. Outside, the air feels tight, or maybe it's me. Between the crowd and the cars, there's an undercurrent that has me tempted to look up at the surrounding buildings.

Chester is closing in on the Gardaí car. They open the door to the back of the squad car.

My chest tightens as I fear that Warren lied to me. Layla speaks to Evelyn about the ruling, and I'm half listening as I watch Chester. This can't be happening. Warren lied to me.

A scream starts off to our right, and on instinct, I reach for Layla and drag her behind me. She squeals in surprise, and I keep my hand clamped on her forearm as I watch through the gaps in the crowd.

A man with his face hooded approaches Chester, the gun in his hand raised. Both Gardaí extract stun guns. The edge of the crowd notices the gunman, and more people join in panicked screams. The tasers are useless weapons, but the Gardaí don't get to fire them, as the gunman empties a round of bullets into Chester's head. Each loud bang of the gun seems violent.

Pop. Pop. Pop.

The screams and chaos that ensue are numbing. I still have Layla behind me when running people slam into me. A burly gentleman crashes into my shoulder hard, and it's enough to make me move as I drag Layla for cover behind a car. She's not screaming or crying like most people. She's staring at me with a look of pure horror in her eyes.

"Stay down," I warn her as I stand up to see the gunman being taken to the ground by the power of two stun guns. He's disarmed and cuffed in seconds, but the screams continue as Chester's body is visible to everyone. Blood pools around the crown of his head, and my mind goes back to the moment with my father.

I can see him so clearly in my mind, blood pooling from his sliced wrists. I stood in it, confused and terrified, until my mother took me from the room.

"Where is she?" Evelyn's hysterical screech pulls me back to the present, back to the chaos of the moment.

"She's here." My voice is stable, and Evelyn's running toward me. She falls to her knees behind the car and grabs Layla, who's sitting quietly in a complete state of shock. Carl pulls off his tie, and as everyone starts to calm down, there's a void that's filled with soft cries and low whispers.

"Layla. Baby, talk to me." Evelyn brushes Layla's hair away from her face.

"I'm okay." Layla's words are breathy as she blinks as if she's just waking up.

Sirens wail in the distance, and I continue to watch everything unfold as more Gardaí cars and an ambulance arrive on site. I don't take my eyes off the damage I did. Not until they lift Chester onto a stretcher. A white sheet covers him, and it soaks up his blood as they place the stretcher in the back of the ambulance and close the doors.

The area is cordoned off with red-and-white tape. A white sheet is erected in seconds and forensics arrive. The gunman's weapon is collected, and I curse Warren, wondering what kind of donkey he hired to take out Chester. I didn't expect someone to shoot him point-blank in the head.

My attention is drawn to Layla as she finally stands. She still wears a dazed look as she looks around the space. "Ashley," Layla says with anguish twisting her features.

Layla moves from behind the car even against Evelyn's cries.

"The gunman is gone." Carl tries to reassure his wife, but I follow Layla as she goes to Ashley and pulls her into her arms. I'm a few feet away and decide I'm close enough to keep an eye on Layla.

My father steps up beside me, and I wish he didn't look so unaffected. "One less to feed in prison. I'm sure they can think of better ways to spend our tax money. Maybe fix some of the potholes on the Monalty road."

"Why are you speaking to me?" I face my father and open the top two buttons of my shirt before loosening my tie.

"Are you still sulking? I got him put away for ten years for you and Layla," he says with pride.

"I got him put down for good," I whisper.

My father's features grow slack. "You." His gaze travels to the pool of blood that's still partially visible under the white sheeting. "This is what you were doing with Warren O'Reagan."

My father looks around the courtyard. "How foolish of you. How foolish of you both." He walks away looking haunted.

I'm still left shocked that Chester was shot at such close range, and the shooter is now in custody. This could go very wrong. For Warren, maybe. I take a second look around the space before I approach Layla.

"I think we should go." I shove my hands into my pockets so I don't reach out and touch her.

"I'm not leaving her." Layla widens her gaze at me while she keeps an arm around a sobbing Ashley's shoulder.

"Do you have anyone to take you home?" I ask Ashley and try to keep my irritation at bay.

Ashley sniffles and looks up like it's the first time she's seen me. "I'll find a way."

"No. We'll drop you home." Layla smiles kindly at Ashley, who nods in acceptance.

I'm left with Ashley as Layla goes over to Carl and Evelyn. I'm expecting Ashley to change her mind and grab a taxi, but she stays close to me with her arms folded across her chest. Her head is bowed as she waits for Layla to return.

"Are you ready?" I ask Layla when she walks back to us.

"Yes. Let's go." Layla takes Ashley's arm, and they walk in front of me. We pass the spot where Chester was shot. Most people have given their statements about what happened, and just when I think we'll get away, we're stopped by two Gardaí.

I feel the color drain from my face even as I tell myself to remain calm.

CHAPTER TWENTY-THREE

JARED

T HE GARDAÍ ASK US about what we saw. Ashley and Layla go first, and by the time it's my turn to answer questions, I'm more controlled. We're told they may have future questions for us, but for now, we can leave.

"I could get a taxi," Ashley says from the back seat. I think it's a great idea, but Layla doesn't.

"Don't be silly. We don't mind." Layla glances at Ashley in the rearview mirror.

"How are you? I mean…" Ashley trails off.

"I'm fine. I don't think anyone is walking away unaffected." Layla meets my gaze.

"Take the next left," Ashley says, her voice distant.

I can't wait to have her out of my car. My skin feels tight, and I reach up to unbutton my shirt but remember it's already opened.

With my foot pressed on the brake, I drop down a gear, indicate, and take the next left.

"He came out of nowhere," Ashley says, her shock still lingering.

"I just heard the bang." Layla wrings her hands in her lap.

I want to say that he deserved to die, but I don't think my words would be appreciated. A large stone archway greets us as I drive into the park.

"Number seven," Layla says. To think she babysat here, and Chester had belittled her, makes me want to get away from this place.

I pull up at the designated parking spot, but I don't kill the engine.

"Will you come in?" Ashley asks.

No. I'm waiting for Layla to say no.

"We would love to." Layla unbuckles her belt, and I'm hoping Ashley will give us a moment, but she sits in the back waiting for Layla.

I switch off the ignition and join them outside.

Layla nods her head at me and gives me a small smile. It softens the edges of her tense features. I relax and take her hand. If this is helping Layla, then I'll go in and make small talk.

Ashley goes ahead of us to the trailer, and we follow behind.

"Hi. How is my little man?" Ashley's voice has shed any earlier upset.

"He's good. You're back early." A young girl's voice floats out the door.

I release Layla's hand so she can go in first, and I follow her. The trailer is small and creaks as we all step in. A young girl, maybe fourteen, is sitting on the floor cross-legged, playing with a baby. I move around them and sit down on the settee.

"Jessie, you are the best," Ashley pays the young girl, who gets up shyly. She doesn't speak to me or Layla but says her goodbyes to Ashley and the baby.

"Isn't he adorable?" Layla whispers to me as she joins the baby on the floor.

Ashley takes off her jacket and folds it in front of her. She's watching Layla play with the baby on the floor.

"I had the most horrible thought."

Layla looks up at Ashley, who's sitting back on her heels as she waits for Ashley to continue.

"I'm glad he died when Nicco wasn't around. Imagine if he had been here and someone shot him. Or hurt Nicco." Tears roll down Ashley's face. "I know it's a horrible thought, but..." She cries into her hands, and Layla gets up and hugs her.

Nicco plays with his small blocks on the floor, a smile on his chubby face. He has no idea that his father is dead, or that he will never see him again.

I reach up to open my shirt buttons, but my fingers touch the flesh of my neck. I want to ask if anyone else feels hot. Ashley keeps crying, and the baby keeps playing.

I stand, needing air. "I'm going outside."

Layla still holds Ashley but nods her head to me in acknowledgment.

The air outside takes away a small amount of the tightness in my chest, but not enough. I keep looking back at the door, hoping Layla will hurry up and come out.

I take out my phone, tempted to ring Warren and ask him what the fuck had happened. Shooting someone at point-blank range isn't what I paid for. The shooter is in custody, and he's hardly going to keep quiet. I rub my hands down my face when the door opens, and Layla sticks her head out. She glances to either side, and when she looks at me, she steps out.

"Can you come in for a second?"

No.

I step away from my car and jog to Layla. "What's wrong?"

"Ashley is throwing up," Layla opens the door wider. "Will you just stay with Nicco?"

I've never sat with a baby in my life. "Yeah."

"Thank you." Her gratitude runs deeply into her words. I reenter the trailer, and she disappears under an arch, leaving me with Nicco.

He's still playing, still giggling as he attempts to stack blocks. I sit down on the settee, and he notices me. His smile wobbles, and I can tell he's going to cry.

"It's okay." I slowly join him on the floor and stack the blocks for him. "I'm just stacking blocks. No need to cry." I speak while I dismantle the tower of blocks before building it up again. I look at Nicco, who's watching me.

I hold out a block to him. His chubby hands try to take it, but it tumbles to the floor, and he laughs.

"You like that?" I ask and stack two blocks together. I flick them and they tumble down, making Nicco laugh again.

"Okay, I see," I say as I repeat building a tower and knocking it down. My objective is to make Nicco laugh, and I achieve it every time. I'm smiling at him when Ashley and Layla step into the room.

Layla wears a look I've never seen before. I immediately get up.

"Thanks for everything." Ashley folds her arms as she speaks to Layla. "I think I'll go lie down."

"Are you sure you don't want us to stay with Nicco?"

As cute as the kid is, I don't want to be here any longer.

"No, I'll take him with me." Ashley uncrosses her arm and rubs Layla's arm. "I'll text later."

I head for the door and let them say their goodbyes. I hate the guilt that swirls inside me, dragging every justified thought with it. I took a father from a child.

I get into the car and watch Layla as she pulls the trailer door shut behind her. She can't seem to help putting people before herself. Layla gets into the car, and once her door is closed, she leans across and presses a kiss to my cheek. "Thank you for doing that for me."

What would she think if she knew I ordered the kill on Chester?

I start the car. "No problem."

I pull out of the trailer park.

"She's had so much happen lately. My heart breaks for her," Layla says.

"You've had a lot happen to you, too," I remind her.

"I know. But I can't help but wonder if you're responsible."

I tighten my hold on the steering wheel as my heart pounds in my chest. "What do you mean?" I glance at Layla.

She's pissed; her small features tighten. There is no fucking way she could know that I got Chester shot, and even so, I don't think she would be pissed. I think she would be demanding for me to drop her back to Evelyn and Carl's.

"Lucas and Sam. They lost their scholarships. Please, Jared, tell me that wasn't you."

My fingers relax on the steering wheel.

"Oh my God. It was," Layla declares. "How could you?"

"Very easily, actually," I mumble and regret it as Layla turns in her seat, only to have the seat belt restrict her.

"Calm down," I say, not wanting her to hurt herself.

"I can't believe you could do such a thing."

"You're in shock and have had a tough day—"

Layla cuts off my words. "No, Jared. What you did to those boys is wrong. That's all they had. They can't afford to educate themselves." Disgust is evident in Layla's words.

I slow down as we reach the gates to my home. They open slowly.

"I promised Evelyn I'd ring her when I get back to your house to let her know I'm safe," Layla explains as she takes her phone out of her bag.

"I'll have Lucas and Sam reinstated," I say while I put the car into gear and drive up toward the house.

"Promise me." Layla's voice is soft.

I pull into the garage and turn off the engine before facing Layla. "I promise you."

She presses a kiss to my cheek. "Thank you."

I nod. "Ring Evelyn. I'll give you a minute," I say, getting out of the car.

I enter the empty kitchen. I'm not sure who I was expecting to see, but it seems emptier than normal. I take out my phone and text Warren.

We need to talk.

I can't stop picturing Nicco sitting on the floor of the trailer, smiling and stacking blocks. Why did I have to see him? Was it to make me feel like I had actually done something wrong? I hate how much it's eating me up.

"Evelyn is going to lie down," Layla says as she enters the kitchen. "I think today took a lot out of everyone." She puts her handbag on the counter and shakes her head. "Can you believe he's dead? That someone just walked right up to him and shot him?"

Layla's brows pull down, and she continues to shake her head. "I know what I saw, but it's so hard to accept."

"I know." I walk to Layla, and she folds in my arms.

"Why are people so evil?" Layla asks.

"I don't know," I respond as my phone vibrates in my pocket. I slip it out as I hold Layla and read the content over her head. It's Warren.

Yeah, I heard. Meet you at KC?

"I have to leave for an hour."

Layla leaves my arms and looks up at me. "Why?"

I reach out and touch her face. "I have to go to the school to speak to the dean."

"For Lucas and Sam?" A ghost of a smile starts on her face.

"Yes. I'll make it right," I promise her, and it's worth it as she smiles. "I won't be long." I press another kiss to her forehead, then I text Warren back, letting him know I'm on my way.

***

The level of guilt that churns in my system has me pushing my foot to the floor as I speed down the road. Killing Chester didn't give me the happiness I thought it would. I'm left with nothing but regret and guilt for taking a child's father from him. Maybe because I grew up without mine. Bert was the closest thing I had as a father, and he was a piss-poor excuse for one. I'm starting to realize that killing Bert won't give me any happiness, either.

I'm trying to stay in control, even as my system flashes warnings telling me that I'm overwhelmed. I take a sharp right onto the college grounds and pull up beside Warren. I unlock the passenger door, and he climbs in. He's wearing a shiner. I accept the fist bump.

I don't say anything but wait for him to start.

"No matter what, you aren't getting a refund." Warren lights up a cigarette. "Not that you need it."

"He walked up to Chester and shot him in the fucking face," I blurt out.

"I heard it was some show, and you had a front-row seat." Warren rolls down the window and flicks out his ashes.

"Are you fucking serious?" I'm trying to keep the anger at bay. Why am I feeling like this?

"That wasn't my guy, Jay," Warren says. "My sniper was on the roof and never got to take the shot. But he did show up for the job, so no refunds."

I slump back in the seat. "I didn't kill Chester," I say to the roof of the car.

"I heard it was a revenge killing. The guy who did it got paid well, and he won't be in prison for long. He's part of a rival gang." Warren claps me on the arm, startling me. "You didn't even have to hire anyone in the end."

He has no idea what all this means to me. "Yeah," I answer.

He inhales a few drags of his cigarette before throwing it out the window, then he laughs. "You must think we're amateurs to shoot someone at close range."

I'm shaking my head, but my mind has left this conversation. I didn't kill Chester. It wasn't my fault. "I thought it odd," I say offhandedly.

"How is Layla?" Warren asks.

That gets my fucking attention, and when I look at him, he grins. "I'm not going to touch your woman."

"I'd hate to have to really beat you up," I say. "You know I held back." The truth tumbles from my mouth. Maybe realizing I didn't kill Chester is giving me some courage.

"I know. But next time, don't." Warren holds out his fist.

"Next time?" I question.

He sneers while tapping my fist with his. "We're good?" he asks.

"Yeah, we're good."

He gets out of the car, and I'm ready to leave but remember my promise to Layla. It doesn't take long with the dean, and the boys will be reinstated by the end of the day. I'm feeling lighter with each step I take to my car, only to stop halfway down the path.

What the actual fuck?

My mother is waiting by my car again.

"I'm not in the mood, Maura," I say as I start walking again.

"I was hoping I could show you something," she says.

"Keep hoping and wishing, because I've somewhere to be." I unlock my car.

"Please. Just give me a lift, and I'll leave you alone."

Maybe it's the day's events that have me considering it. "A lift to where?"

"If I told you, you wouldn't believe me."

Fuck it.

"No. You're pissing me off again." I get into the car, done with her shit.

"To the graveyard." She knocks on the passenger side. "I promise, you do this and I'll leave you alone."

She's holding my gaze. The graveyard is only on the outskirts of town. I want to ask her who's buried there, but instead, I pop the lock and she quickly climbs in.

"Thank you so much," she says.

"You'll leave me alone after this? No more showing up at my home or school?"

She nods. "Yes."

I start the car and leave the school grounds while texting Layla, telling her I'll be home in a few minutes. I don't like her being alone.

"You shouldn't be on the phone while driving," Maura says.

"I never said you could talk." I put my phone away.

"The memory you had as a boy of your father in the bathroom? That was real."

I narrow my eyes at Maura. "Fucking stop. I checked his wrists. There isn't a blemish on them. So stop fucking lying. Now shut up, or I'll drop you off on the side of the road." My threat should have her going silent, but it doesn't.

"He's not your father. He's your uncle."

I jam on the breaks. "Get out."

"Listen to me. He's your uncle. Your father had an identical twin. And when your father took his life, your uncle took his place."

I'm sitting in my car listening to this crackpot. I exhale loudly and try to remain calm. "Get out." I speak low.

"He did it for the money, Jared. But he didn't know that when either I or your father died, everything went to you. Nothing can be transferred until you're twenty-two. That's what he'll ask you to sign in a week. It's not so you can inherit everything. It's so you will transfer everything back to him. Your father made it in his will. We both did."

My heart roars in my ears, and I don't know what to make of my mother's words. "Why did you put me in the foster system?" I ask.

"To hide you. To keep you safe from him. I feared he might kill you."

I face my mother. "Why not take me with you?"

"We had to separate." My mother reaches for my hand. "You have no idea what he is capable of."

"I have no idea what you're capable of. Right now, Maura, this sounds like a crock of shit." I pretend that her words have no effect on me, but sadly, they do.

"I can show you your father's grave."

"Get out of my car." I rub my temples like I can dispel the confusion her words are causing.

"William knows the truth. He's always looked out for you."

"If he's my uncle, how could he pose as my father? What about social security?" I'm asking questions, but I really feel that money can get you anything.

"I don't know how he convinced the child protective services to hand you over. I just know he did."

She's pleading with her eyes, and I want to believe her, but it's too farfetched. Yet, my gut won't settle. Nothing in me will settle, and I know I won't either until I have the truth.

"This is my final time telling you this, Maura. Get out of my car."

Tears stream down her face, and she finally unbuckles her belt. "Just talk to William" are her departing words as she gets out of the car.

CHAPTER TWENTY-FOUR

LAYLA

J ARED TEXTED SAYING HE would be home in a few minutes. That was two hours ago. I've changed out of my court clothes and swapped them for yoga pants and an oversized green sweater. After slipping on my tennis shoes, I leave my room and knock on Jared's bedroom door before entering. No one is here. His bed is made; his room immaculate.

I leave and make my way through the large hallway. Kerry smiles at me as she passes. "Anything I can do for you?"

"Have you seen Jared?" I ask.

Her smile slowly fades. "No. Shall I look for him?"

I wave her off. "No, thanks. That's okay, Kerry."

The kitchen is empty, and I check the garage. I'm surprised when I spot the BMW that Jared has been driving since his own car is at the garage for repair. I close the garage door and return to the house. I find my feet moving toward the staircase, but I pause on the first step. If he is up there, maybe I should give him some space.

I take my foot off the step and walk down the opposite hall. I haven't explored this side of the house. The doors that line either side of the wall are numerous.

"What do you want?" Jared's words are spoken harshly—a sharpness I'm sure would be visible on his face if I could see him.

I step closer to the half-open door.

"Just a minute of your time, son." Athar says the word 'son' as if he's leaning into it. I don't know him very well, but I can imagine his lips tightening around the word.

I push the door open more and see Jared's back is to me. His hands hang on either side of him, and his shoulders seem tense. Athar has his back to me, too, so I feel safe in my position as I watch them. I should announce that I'm here, but something holds me back.

"I have some paperwork I thought we could sign today, as my solicitor sent it over before the court case."

Jared snorts, his hands rolling into fists. "Is this for my inheritance?"

"Yes." Athar turns and sees me. His gaze hardens, and I try to move out of his line of sight, but it's too late. Jared turns, and I'm ready to explain why I'm standing here listening.

"Layla, come on in."

I take a hesitant step into the room. "I was worried about you," I say.

It's awkward as I walk across the floor to Jared.

"Don't you think it best to let Layla rest while we talk business?" Athar says as he walks to a large desk that dominates the space.

I'm ready to run from the room. I'd gladly give them space, but Jared shakes his head.

"Actually, I'd like Layla here."

Athar narrows his eyes briefly before relaxing back into his seat. "Very well." He opens a folder on his desk and takes out some paperwork. "I'm sure Layla will want to celebrate also."

Jared steps toward his father's desk.

"Celebrate what?" I ask.

"Why, Jared's inheritance."

I grow uncomfortable. "Only if Jared wants me here," I say and try not to pull at my sweater.

"I do." Jared speaks with his back to me as he picks up the paperwork. "If you had asked me to sign this a few hours ago, I would have been asking for a pen. But..." Jared places the paperwork on the desk. "I don't think I'm ready for the business."

"Nonsense. You are ready. You're my son." Athar stands with his shoulders back, and I get that feeling like I'm intruding on a tender moment. I glance away and take in the rows of bookshelves that are mounted to the wall.

Jared exhales loudly. "No, I'm not."

I take a peek as Jared slides the paperwork back to his father. Athar's lips form an angry, thin line, and color soaks into his cheeks.

"I want you to have it, son. Sign today, sign tomorrow. It won't matter. It will be yours. You don't have to start work straight away. I understand there will be a transition period."

"What if it's already mine?" Jared asks and his words are low, deadly.

Athar flinches, and I startle as the door opens behind me. William arrives carrying a file in his hand. Or maybe it's a large envelope.

"What do you want, William?" Athar bites. I've never heard him raise his voice before.

I wrap my arms around my waist. I want Jared to just sign the papers so we can leave.

"I was a loyal servant of Brian's," William starts. "He was a good man. I knew one day the truth would come out, and I swore to Maura that I would be here to bring the secrets into the light."

"What are you spouting on about?" Athar stands up from his chair, but he's visibly shaken. I have no idea what's going on.

"There was so much I couldn't piece together. Like the memory of my father dying in the bathroom."

"Not this again." Athar moves around the desk.

"You will listen to me." Jared's roar has my heart stalling in my chest. I think even the air stills with fear.

Athar pauses, the color draining from his face.

"My father is dead. And you are an imposter." Jared's words leave me reeling.

"Prove it." Athar stands straight, with his shoulders back.

William steps closer and hands Jared a file.

"At school, one of my friends asked Warren O'Reagan about his uncle's once owning the castle." Jared paces as he speaks. "I mean, I knew it was ours, so when Warren said they still owned it, I was surprised."

Jared stops moving as he faces his father. "I asked Warren about it today, and he told me that the O'Reagan's forged documents for you." Jared fires the file at Athar. It hits his chest, and pages flutter to the floor.

Anger flushes Athar's skin, and I take a step back.

"You didn't care about what Warren and I were up to. You were worried I might get close enough for him to tell me all about your seedy dealings." Jared takes a step toward Athar with his fists tightened.

"What about you? You had Chester shot. How will people feel when they know the lunatic you are?" Athar looks at me. "How will Layla feel?"

I take another step back, and I'm shaking my head. Jared turns, and his gaze is so full of anger that it halts my steps.

"No. You wouldn't do that to Chester." I'm praying that this isn't true.

Jared deflates immediately. "No, I didn't."

My head spins as Jared looks back to his father. "What happened to Chester was from a rival gang."

"Lies," Athar shouts and he's a drowning man.

Jared steps around Athar and picks up the documents that Athar wanted him to sign only moments ago. "What are these papers for?"

Athar doesn't answer. I'm holding my breath, and when Jared launches himself at Athar, I'm frozen as his fist slams into his father's face. William rushes forward to stop Jared, but Jared swings and sends William sailing back onto the ground.

I race to William to help him up. "Are you okay?" I ask.

William nods his head. I turn to Jared, who has Athar on the ground, and his fist smashes into Athar's face.

"Did you kill my father?" Jared roars, but even if Athar wanted to answer, Jared doesn't give him the opportunity.

"Stop it." I get up off the floor and run to Jared. "Stop it."

His violence pours out of him, and this isn't the boy I remember. My heart seems to shatter as I watch Jared lose himself in the rage that is powering him. I saw it with Kieran, and now I see it again with Jared and his father. I grip Jared's arm.

"What's going on? This isn't you. You're not violent." He doesn't look at me but stares down at Athar, who is bleeding from his mouth and nose.

"He's not my father."

I'm starting to see that nothing is what it seemed here. "I believe you."

His head whips up, a muscle tightening in his jaw.

"But the rage, it's making you into something you're not," I say.

He snorts with anger and releases Athar, who groans on the floor. "You have no idea."

Snakes coil in my stomach at his words. The silence that follows is deafening.

"What aren't you telling me?" I finally say it out loud and can feel the full extent of Jared's stare on me. But I can't look away from him, and fear has me trying to claw my words back. I'm going to lose him. He looks like a man possessed as he pulls at his shirt. His hands touch his neck, and I reach out to him. "What's happening?"

"Nothing."

His one word has tears running down my face.

Everything.

I cling to the moment as my heart bounces around in my chest.

"You're lying." My words have him jumping off the floor.

"I can't fucking breathe." Jared walks to William. "Don't let him out of your sight. The Gardaí are on their way," Jared tells William, who nods.

Before I can react, Jared starts to run from the room. He never runs or hides from me. My legs propel me forward, and I'm chasing after Jared.

"Talk to me!" I scream at him as he runs for the front door. He glances at me over his shoulder, and I've never seen such fear in someone's eyes. Jared pauses as he opens the front door to the onslaught of rain. I'm waiting for him to stop, but he runs out into the pounding rain. I don't pause and ignore the rain.

"What aren't you telling me?" I scream at his back. Jared freezes.

"What aren't you telling me?" I demand again. Jared stands still, breathing heavily in the rain. Something about his stance reminds me of a cornered animal.

"Today, I feel like I don't even know you."

Rain falls heavier; each drop feels so full and cold as I wait for Jared to answer.

"You know me."

I'm shaking my head as he speaks. "Not all of you. Not that person in there. You are so angry. Jesus. I've seen it before with Kieran." I turn away, my clothes soaked right through.

I don't fully understand what took place in his home with Athar, but something made me feel this isn't really about that. I think I've been avoiding the truth for a long time.

"Fine. I'll tell you," Jared whispers.

I hear him and my soul shivers. I'm finally going to find out.

CHAPTER TWENTY-FIVE

LAYLA

J ARED'S CHEST RISES AND falls rapidly. "He's not my father."

I'm shaking my head. "You know what I'm asking."

I wasn't asking about Athar or anything else. I'm finally asking why Jared, who was always a peacekeeper while we were growing up, has turned into someone who is so violent. I recognize pain, and maybe I was too scared of the answer before. Maybe I'm at a breaking point with everything that has happened. Maybe I'm tired of turning a blind eye.

"I used to go into your room at night to steal your sweater," I say. "Why was Bert leaving your room?" It was a memory from when I was a child, yet the image of Bert coming out of Jared's bedroom always haunted me. Tears mix with rain, and I want to scream into the air.

"Bert hurt me too." The whispered words have me moving closer to Jared, in case I miss one word. He's staring at the ground, his fists clenched. I stop moving when he looks up at me. I've often heard the phrase that there's a storm brewing in someone's eyes, but I never understood the meaning until right now, looking at Jared.

His irises dilate, consuming the brown and turning them black. Anger flashes, then a sparkle of gold splashes across them. The brown lightens until all the color is gone, and only sadness, hurt, and pain are left. Some part of me knows he's been hurt in a way no one ever should be.

My eyes burn as I stare at Jared. Swallowing, I swipe at droplets of rain on my cheek. Jared's hair darkens as the rain continues to pelt down on top of us.

"Like he hurt me?" I ask. The tension that enters Jared's frame is at a snapping point, and some part of me wants him to snap. I want him to crumble and let it all out.

His jaw clenches as he works a muscle in his jaw. He speaks through his teeth. Each word is ground out. "No, not like he hurt you, Layla."

I nod, not sure why I am. He looks away again, his shoulders slumping, crumbling, and I take another step toward him. I'm terrified of what he might say but terrified that he won't say anything either.

The rain falls with more weight, and the volume soaks both of us, but Jared doesn't seem to notice. He's stuck in his own turmoil. I take a final step and stand in front of him.

"Jared."

His head springs up. His eyes are haunted by whatever memory he's having. Something tells me not to touch him, and I listen to the voice.

"Nobody knew." Jared speaks with furrowed brows. "I made sure no one knew."

I'm nodding again, swallowing my fear. My stomach has been twisting and diving since I chased after him. From the moment he had paused at the front door, I felt the dread dripping down my spine. I shiver, not only from the rain but also from the look on Jared's face. The pain inside me is like nothing I've ever known.

"What did he do?" I ask, and my heart plummets.

He doesn't answer me. "Did he touch you?" I whisper, wanting him to tell me that I'm crazy. That I'm wrong.

But he nods, not looking at me.

The ground shifts under my feet, and Jared reaches out, grabbing me around the waist, stopping me from hitting the ground. Pain roars through me, blocking out sound briefly before it comes crashing back.

"Now you know all of me," he says with an emptiness in his voice.

That is more frightening than anything I've ever heard before. My mind races with so many questions. Like, why didn't he tell someone? How long did it go on? Oh God, how far did it go?

I want to bawl for him, for Jared. I want to kill Bert. I hated him before, but now, thinking of what he did to Jared...

The things I wanted to do to him before now seem like nothing. Knowing what I know now, I want him to suffer. I feel sick. My heart pounds at the injustice, but I know Jared and right now, looking at him, he needs me. He still holds me, his grip solid, and I reach up, taking his face in my hands.

"I love you, Jared. All. Of. You." My lips touch his cold and stiff ones, but after a moment, he kisses me back. The agony of knowing he's hurting feels so real, and I want a morphine drip to stop the pain. How must he feel?

Blue and red lights catch droplets of rain before they expand, and the world is blanketed in the lights of the Gardaí car that makes its way up the driveway.

The front door is still open, and William is standing, watching us, and I wonder how much he heard.

"Jay McGivney?" A Ban-Gardaí walks toward us. Holding her hat down over her head like it might keep her dry. Her waterproof clothes shine with the falling rain.

I'm not sure how aware Jared is of his surroundings.

"The man you want is in the house," William calls from the front door.

The second Gardaí joins the Ban-Gardaí, and they follow William inside.

They all disappear through the curtain of rain. I entwine my fingers with Jared's, but he pulls against me.

"What are you doing?" he asks, and I stop tugging.

"Please, trust me?" I say.

He nods and I kiss him softly on the lips before resuming our walk toward the house. William left the front door open. Commotion down the hall has Jared pulling his hand out of mine.

"This is ludicrous," Athar yells.

"Athar McGivney, you're being arrested for identity theft, fraud offenses, and embezzlement. You are not obliged to say anything unless you wish to do so, but whatever you say will be taken down in writing and may be given in evidence."

Handcuffs are placed around Athar's wrists, and it's all starting to sink in that this man isn't Jared's father. Athar pulls against his cuffs as he approaches us, and I find myself stepping in front of Jared.

"You won't get away with this," he snarls.

"All they have to do is a blood test. Everyone will know the truth of who you are." Jared's words are flat.

Athar is taken from the house by the Ban-Gardaí. The Gardaí stops in front of us.

"How long have you been standing out in the rain? You're soaked." The Gardaí looks from me to Jared. When I glance back at Jared, he looks so haunted and dazed. I don't want any more questions fired at him. He's been through enough.

"I lost my purse. We were looking for it," I say. The lights bounce around the foyer, and I just want the Gardaí to leave.

Maybe he senses it as he looks at Jared. "We'll be in touch." He leaves and William closes the door behind him.

The cold settles fast and hard.

"I'll get you some towels," William says while walking away, and it gives me a moment with Jared.

He stuffs his hands into the pockets of his jeans as water drips off him.

William returns, handing me a stack of towels.

"Thank you, William." I hold them to my chest.

"If you need anything else…" William doesn't finish his sentence but takes a worrying glance at Jared before leaving us alone.

"I think you should go home." Some emotion has entered Jared's words.

I'm shaking my head, already expecting this from him. "I need you." I allow the pain to enter my voice. It works like I knew it would, and I don't feel guilty.

Jared reaches out, and I hand him a towel. He starts to dry himself off.

"I should go to the Gardaí station." Jared speaks as he pulls off his shirt.

I'm shaking my head as I grab my hair and pat it between the towels. "Jared, you can face all that tomorrow. Tonight, I need you."

We dry in silence, and when Jared reaches for me, I grip his hand while my emotions skyrocket. It's like all his pain is transferred in that small touch. We walk to his room, and with each step, his features continue to tighten.

Once we're in his room, Jared strips off the rest of his clothes. He's standing still, holding the key in his hand. He's lost in his thoughts, and pain tears through me as tears roll down his face. I'm frozen, broken, as my chest threatens to cave in. Jared takes the key from around his neck and places it on the top of the chest of drawers. He half looks at me before going to his walk-in wardrobe. With him out of sight, my heart palpitates, and I take quick, deep breaths.

Don't cry, Layla. Don't cry, I chant in my head. Yet tears escape, and I wipe them away quickly as Jared returns dressed in sweatpants and a T-shirt. He hands me sweatpants and a T-shirt as well.

"Thank you." I take them and strip off my wet clothes. I don't bother with the sweatpants but change into the oversized top that floats to my knees. I towel-dry my hair and comb it out with my fingers as Jared walks around his room, scrubbing his face every few minutes. He won't look at me, and when I catch glimpses, his eyes are red and puffy.

I wipe my own tears as I climb up onto his bed. "Get in," I tell him, pulling the blankets back.

Jared stuffs his hands into his pockets. He seems to be considering it, and my heart pounds. I don't want him to be alone tonight, but it's there in his eyes that he wants to leave or send me away.

"Please," I whisper.

His brows furrow. I win. He walks to the bed and lies down beside me. I sit beside him while pulling the blankets up to his knees.

"I remember the first time I told Evelyn about what happened to me. It was the most terrifying thing ever. When she came back the next day, I wanted her to leave. I wanted to take my words back because by saying it, it became real." I touch Jared's face. "But it healed a part of me. It was a small part, but it was a start."

Jared's eyes glisten, and a silent tear runs down the side of his face, and I die a little inside but remain still.

"I won't run from you, Layla. I was afraid you might run from me." His honest words stab at me, and my eyes and throat burn. My body has never felt so taut, so hell-bent on snapping. All the tension is at the breaking point.

"I love you. I'm here for the good and bad. Always." I kiss him gently on the lips before lying down beside him.

Deep circles darken under his haunted eyes, and I rub his cheek, letting my hand trail into his hair. The exhaustion has his eyelashes touching his cheeks. I caress his hair until his breathing evens out, and I know he's asleep.

***

I barely sleep, and every time Jared moves, I wake up, afraid he'll leave. But he sleeps the whole night through. His breathing isn't as even now, telling me he's waking up. I pull my arms tight against my body, and he stares at me. A smile spreads across his face, his arm reaching out until he captures me around the waist. A small squeal escapes my lips as he pulls me to him and buries his head in the crook of my neck.

"I could smell you," he says, his warm breath causing goose bumps to break out along my skin. It isn't the reception I expected, but for just this moment, I won't complain. His nibbles on my neck have me choking a laugh.

"Good morning." Brown eyes still half-closed with sleep stare at me as a lazy smile hangs from his lips. His tongue flicks out to moisten them.

"Good morning." I lean in and kiss him, his eyes widening before closing as he deepens the kiss.

A knock on the bedroom door has us breaking apart. Jared wakes up fully and gets out of bed. The heaviness of last night returns with each step he takes. The transformation has his shoulders tensing.

"Good morning, William." As Jared speaks, he opens the door fully. Jared runs his hands through his hair.

"Master Jay. Breakfast is ready."

Jared nods. "We will be there in a moment." Jared doesn't close the door, and when William's gaze lands on me, I give him a half smile. He bows his head before leaving. Jared returns to the edge of the bed and reaches across to entwine our fingers together. I'm beginning to think he isn't aware of what he's doing. He just constantly needs to be touching me. I'm not complaining, but it's distracting.

"How did you sleep?" he asks.

"Good," I reply.

Jared rubs his jaw. "You look tired."

"So do you." I shuffle closer to him. "We need to talk about last night."

Jared releases my hand while running his fingers through his hair. "Not now. I need to eat first." He stands, not looking at me. I knew it would be a sensitive topic, but I don't want it ignored and buried again.

"I'm going to get dressed," I say to Jared, understanding that now isn't the time.

Jared goes to his walk-in wardrobe to get dressed, and I pause, tempted to follow him in there and make him face what he told me last night. But, I need to have patience. I leave him and go to my room. Kerry is standing outside the door.

"You can take the day off, Kerry," I say, knowing that the entire staff isn't necessary.

She folds her hands in front of her. "Are you sure?"

"Positive, and the same for Andrea and Amanda."

Kerry bows her head before leaving, and I dress mechanically, hating not being with Jared. I don't want him to flee. I dress in record time and make my way to the dining room. Jared is already there, and I sit across from him, where William places a full Irish breakfast in front of me.

"Thank you, William," I say.

"You are very welcome."

"I have to go to the Gardaí station this morning." Jared's plate is still full. He holds the knife and fork and pushes a sausage on his plate.

"After you eat," I say.

He forces a smile, but it's a shadow of what I'm used to.

"William will drive you to Evelyn and Carl's. You should spend some time with them today."

I'm already shaking my head. William hasn't left, but I don't hold back. "No, I'll wait here for you, Jared."

"I'll be gone most of the day, Layla. I have to go to the Gardaí and my solicitor." Jared's features soften. "I'll pick you up later. Please do this for me."

"Okay." I give in, knowing staying here all day isn't something I want to do, and I also know Jared needs to get his affairs in order.

Jared rises and walks around the table. He stops and presses a kiss on the crown of my head.

"Jared, we need to chat later," I remind him. I can't bear for him to shut me out.

"Yeah," he mumbles and then he's gone.

CHAPTER TWENTY-SIX

LAYLA

I DON'T LINGER AFTER Jared leaves, and William drops me home. I let myself in but stand staring at the door I closed behind me. My throat burns when I finally let what Jared told me sink in. My mind races through every memory, every moment, looking for signs, and the sad thing is, they were there. I cover the sob that forces its way up my throat. Bert had hit all of us—except Jared and Nelson. My heart pounds. Is that why Nelson killed himself? My eyes burn, and my vision wavers.

"Layla."

I squeeze my eyes shut when I hear Evelyn's voice. She's standing behind me, distraught and confused, and yet I don't know what to tell her. I try to push down my emotions. My face is still wet as I turn to her.

"Do you want to talk about it?" she asks softly, her head tilting to the side.

I pull down the sleeves of my top over my fingers. "Yes. But I can't."

She nods. "Did something happen between you and Jared?"

I wipe my nose with my sleeve. "No. Just something happened to him." My lip and voice tremble.

"Something you can't tell me," Evelyn says.

"No." My voice cracks, and then I'm in Evelyn's arms. Her hand rubs my hair like she's done for years. "I love him," I say.

"I know you do, sweetheart."

"I'm scared." This time, Evelyn makes me face her.

"Of what?" As Evelyn searches my face, her concern isn't coming from my therapist but from my mother.

"Of losing him again." Tears fall fast and hard. This time, I can't control them. Evelyn pulls me back into her arms.

"That boy loves you. He's not going anywhere."

I stop talking after that because that isn't what I meant. Evelyn, being the amazing mother she is, doesn't question me any further.

I take a shower before getting my phone out to text Jared, but I already have a message from him. My heart beats fast as I open the message. My stomach twists painfully. What if he's going to push me away?

I'm nearly done. Can I pick you up in an hour?

"Okay. Okay." I'm nodding as I speak out loud and write back: **Okay**.

This is a good sign. I get dressed in a long skirt, flip-flops, and a tank top. The day is already heating up. Tying my hair up, I arrive back downstairs. Evelyn is out in the backyard on our swing chair. The sliding door is open, and I step out into the hot day. Smoke billows around her, and the smell of cigarettes burns my nose. I've never seen Evelyn or Carl smoke; the minute Evelyn sees me, she drops her hand to her side, trying to hide the cigarette, but smoke still billows upwards.

"Since when do you smoke?" I ask, sitting beside her. She lifts the cigarette as if she's never seen it before, and I raise an eyebrow.

"Just sometimes," she says quickly before inhaling again. It's such a strange thing to see her do.

"What times call for a cigarette?" I ask, hating that I have worried her enough to smoke.

"Nothing for you to worry about." Her smile doesn't reach her eyes.

"I know you see me as a kid. But I'm here for you, too," I tell her.

Her eyes sparkle. "I don't see you as a kid, Layla." She rubs my face with her free hand. "You are a young woman, and I just hope I did enough." Her brows knit together. "That I made the right decisions along the way."

"Evelyn, you're the best mother ever," I tell her, and her tears fall, but she wipes them away quickly before inhaling her cigarette. Something tells me she's building herself up.

"When we found out that Nelson died, I did some digging," she says, then she throws the cigarette on the ground. Beads of sweat break out on my forehead.

"Ronnie came forward with information against Bert." Evelyn looks at me, and my heart pounds in my ears. I'm holding Evelyn's arm. I didn't realize I even moved.

"He abused Nelson," she says quietly. My lip trembles as I watch tears fall from Evelyn's eyes. "I have been your therapist for seven years, and I don't know how I missed this." And there it is: all her fear, all her guilt pouring out. All of it is unnecessary. She looks crushed as she glances up at me. "I'm so sorry."

I'm shaking my head, still holding on to her. "I wasn't... He didn't hurt me like that." Pain claws its way up my throat as I think of Jared. A part of me feels worse because it's Jared who has been hurt. My mind is conjuring up horrific scenes, and the worst part is, most likely, they're all real. I press my hand to my chest, trying to push the pain down.

"What he did to me has damaged me so much, Evelyn, but what he did to those boys..." Tears roll down my face. "I feel like when I think of Jared, I can't breathe." Anger has me clamping my teeth together as I cry. Evelyn moves closer, pulling me to her. No words are said as she rocks me, and I feel so selfish to grieve when I haven't suffered like the boys. Jared and Nelson did.

"I used to pray for Bert and Ronnie that they would stop hurting people." I sit back and wipe angrily at my face. "Now I hope they die a horrible and painful death."

"Shh." Evelyn's tears fall as she tries to settle me. I can feel hysteria tingeing my words, but speaking about it is letting out all the anger and upset.

We sit in each other's arms. Evelyn rubs my hair, but the worry around her eyes is gone with the knowledge that I wasn't harmed like that and that she didn't fail me. For me, I want to be strong when Jared picks me up. I want all the tears out so I can be his rock. I don't want him to hold me and soothe me. I want it to be about him.

When we finally let each other go, I'm still feeling tender, and by the drawn look on Evelyn's face, so is she.

"Jared's picking me up soon."

Evelyn nods at my words as she fixes my hair behind my ear.

"He had to go to the Gardaí station about Athar. He isn't Jared's father. He's his uncle, pretending to be his father."

I'm not sure how much more Evelyn can take. I'm not sure how much any of us can take, but I tell her everything that happened at Jared's.

"Athar seemed so nice, so considerate of Jared." Evelyn shakes her head. "I can't believe he's not his father. I'm shocked."

"It will take a long time to sink in," I say.

"Carl and I are here for both of you. You and Jared."

"Thank you, Evelyn," I whisper, closing my eyes tight just for a moment. Her words mean everything to me.

Jared was abused. How did I not notice? How did so many social workers that checked up on us not notice? Then again, I hid my own abuse so I wouldn't be separated from Jared. He was all I'd ever known; he was my safe feeling in a dangerous place. Now, the knowledge that it was far darker than I ever could have imagined leaves me feeling lost.

"If Jared needs to talk." Evelyn trails off at the look of horror on my face. "Not me, but I have lots of contacts."

I relax. I don't want my boyfriend telling my mother all his secrets and pain.

"Thanks." I manage a smile. My phone vibrates in my pocket, and I pull it out.

I'm outside.

It's from Jared. My stomach feels empty. Like that horrible, empty feeling you get when you go to bed without dinner and each hunger pain wakes you up. I get up off the swinging bench, pushing down another childhood memory.

"Jared's outside."

Evelyn gets up and hugs me tightly.

"Please don't forget that we're here for both of you," she tells me.

It eases my anxiety a bit, knowing that we aren't alone.

I quickly wash my face and grab my bag. Jared is parked in the drive, his head bowed as he looks at something in his hands. Closing the front door, he looks up. Against the horror of what is happening, I smile, knowing that everything will be alright. I have Jared, after all.

The smile that spreads across his face has me walking faster toward the car. His brown eyes never leave me, and I know there and then that I'm the luckiest person in the world.

Climbing in, I don't give him a second but take his face in my hands and kiss him. My life has been hard, his life has been harder, but I want the past to remain the past and focus on the future. It won't just be my future, but my and Jared's.

"I love you," I whisper against his lips.

His eyes flicker up to mine, his breath brushing my lips. "I love you too, Layla."

I smile into our next kiss, which is soft and short.

We drive in a silence that isn't awkward. I'm mentally preparing myself for what will come next. Maybe he is, too. Jared drives to the beach where the party took place. The day is warm, and when we pull up, we get out without saying anything. I know walking and talking about such a heavy topic will be easier than sitting in a tin can. Jared walks around the car and entwines our fingers together. There's a brief moment when a look passes between us. It's like we're both in agreement that we can do this. That we have to do this.

We remove our shoes and walk along the shoreline. Waves brush against my feet. The feel of water and sand is making me feel more grounded.

"Are you okay?" I start it off with a stupid question, but one that opens up the large black stage to its first victim. Jared, never one to hide, smiles at me. I wonder if he knows how brave he is.

"I am. I've sorted out a lot with Athar, but it won't happen overnight. It will take time." He says this as his free hand rubs the back of his neck.

"You're amazing. You know that?" I tell him.

His lips tug slightly as he narrows his eyes. "No, but I could get used to hearing that."

"Great. You're going to hear it every day, forever."

His smile grows as he tugs on my hand. "You always make me feel better." His words are delivered with a pull to my heart, and silence falls between us again. Pain tears at my heart every time I think of him being hurt. I stop walking, wanting to look at him.

"What can I do?" I ask.

His jaw tightens, but he doesn't shy away from me. "Just be here, be patient."

"Always."

Jared starts to walk again. "I was terrified to tell you, but I knew I had to."

I'm staring at Jared in awe. He is amazing. He is perfect. He is mine.

"Thank you for trusting me." We stop again, and Jared moves closer, sending my heart pounding. The effect he has on me is frightening at times, and the way he looks at me now, like I'm the most important person in the world, has my breaths coming in short puffs.

"You're the only person I trust. You always have been." Jared's arm snakes around my waist as he pulls me into his arms.

I close my eyes and inhale deeply. I love him so much. The more we talk, the more I love him.

"What happens now?" I ask against his chest, staring out at the ocean.

"Right now? Like this second?" I can hear the laugh in his voice, and I smile into his chest.

"Don't be a smartass," I say, leaning back from him as his dimples appear.

"It's cute when you swear," he says before planting a kiss on my nose.

I wiggle my nose, and he laughs. "'Ass' isn't a curse," I declare.

"It's still cute." We smile at each other as the waves break at our feet.

"We'll be fine." Jared's words are said with such assurance that I believe him.

"Of course we will. We have each other."

EPILOGUE

LAYLA

I 'D LIKE TO SAY we walked off into the sunset like I've seen in so many movies, but that's not what happened. We continued to grow and heal together. People say time is a great healer, and it is. But no wound ever fully heals. I think you just learn to live with your demons. They have a special corner in your head. A corner they stick to most of the time.

The court case against Bert arrives, and I take the stand, telling the world what I endured at the hands of Bert and Ronnie. It's hard. It's emotional. But I have Jared, Carl, Evelyn, and even Ashley to support me, which means so much. Rex and Jared's mother joined us too.

I've never been prouder than when Jared walks up the aisle to take the stand; I've also never been so terrified.

"I'm so proud of you," I tell Jared once we have a second alone. It's the first day of court, and we have a few more to go. We weren't the only children in Bert and Ronnie's care. The court has a lot of different witnesses to listen to. I just hated the fact that we had to see Bert and Ronnie again. I didn't look at them directly, but I could feel their eyes on me as I took the stand.

"Who's hungry?" Evelyn asks, and Ashley speaks first.

"I'm starving. Where are we going?"

I smile at her.

"There's a small café down the street," Jared's mother announces, and we all agree that will be fine. Evelyn and Carl walk beside me as Jared holds my hand. Maura walks in front of us, with Ashley and Rex following behind us. We're an odd group. But this is us.

These are the people that are important to us, and the ones that will help us through it. I squeeze Jared's hand, three quick times. It's a signal we've started doing when we can't talk. *We'll be okay*—that's what we're saying to each other. I smile when he squeezes my hand back.

Yeah, everything will be okay.

***

WANT TO READ MORE BOOKS LIKE THIS ONE FROM VI CARTER?

CHECK OUT A DEADLY OBSESSION DUET.

Start reading A DEADLY OBSESSION! HERE

Sign up to my newsletter if you want to be notified about my new releases. HERE

ABOUT THE AUTHOR

When Vi Carter isn't writing dark romance books, you can find her reading her favorite authors, baking, taking photos, or watching Netflix.

Married with three children, Vi divides her time between motherhood and all the other hats she wears as an Author.
Social Media Links for Vi Carter

Website

Facebook Reader Group

Facebook Author Page

ACKNOWLEDGEMENTS

I'm very lucky to have such amazing readers and Beta Readers. I want to thank the following people who worked with me on this book.

Developmental Editor: Amanda Cuff
Proofreader: Michele Rolfe
Blurb was written by: Tami Thomason
Proofreader: Amanda Cuff

Beta Readers
Amanda Sheridan
Laura Riley
Lucy Korth
Tami Thomason
Ashley Wheelock